The Story Of Maude Reed

A *Tree of Life* Book

Published by arrangement with the author's Estate.

Copyright © Clive Lofts 2024
First published in Great Britain by Transworld, 1971.
Published in the USA (as *The Maude Reed Tale*)
by Nelson, 1972.

Cover illustration: generated in
Microsoft Designer by Lion

Typed for Tree of Life Publishing by
Elizabeth Walton

A CIP catalogue record for this book is
available from the British Library.

ISBN: 978-1-915816-07-8

Tree of Life Publishing
United Kingdom

The Story Of Maude Reed

Norah Lofts

Also by Norah Lofts from Tree of Life Publishing:

Esther
How Far to Bethlehem?
Jassy
Bless This House
The Devil in Clevely
Scent of Cloves
The Lute Player
The Town House
The House at Old Vine
The House at Sunset
The Lost Queen
Eleanor The Queen: *A Novel of Eleanor of Aquitaine*
Hester Roon
Michael And All Angels
Knight's Acre
The Homecoming
The Lonely Furrow
Charlotte
Gad's Hall/The Haunting of Gad's Hall (as one volume)
The Old Priory
Pargeters
A Wayside Tavern
The Road To Revelation

CHAPTER I

I cried, on and off, for four days when my mother told me that it was all arranged for me to leave home and everybody and everything I loved and go to live in a strange place with people I had never seen.

At first I cried very loudly, so loudly that people came running from all over the house and from the yard to see what had happened to me. I roared, 'I will not go to Beauclaire or anywhere else! Why should I be sent away from home?' I beat on the table with my fists.

'The way you are behaving at this minute,' Mother said coldly, 'is proof that you need some lessons in ladylike behaviour.'

'I do not want to be a lady,' I shouted. 'I want to be a wool merchant.'

'That is ridiculous talk. Who ever heard of a woman wool merchant? You will go to Beauclaire and forget all such nonsense and, I hope, learn some manners.'

I could see that I was doing myself no good, so I cried more quietly and made up my mind to talk to my grandfather, the one person who understood me and had never yet let me down.

This time he did. He was as kind as ever, took me on his knee and said, 'Maude, don't cry; crying never did any good.' But he also said, 'Your mother and I have talked this over and over. I was against the idea myself at first but she has persuaded me that this will be the best thing for you, in the long run.'

'There won't be a long run. I shall die of a broken heart.'

'People don't die of heartbreak,' he said. I knew there had been sadnesses in his life. He never spoke of them himself but running about in the yard and in the woolsheds I had heard gossip. Long ago his first wife and two or three children had been burned to death in a terrible fire. Then he had married again and had one son, my father; the second wife had died and all grandfather's love had been poured out on my father—by all accounts a naughty child, rather like me. But Father had died young, too. So that left Grandfather with me and Walter—we were twins— and you would have thought that after so many losses he would have wanted to hold on to me.

I said, rather cunningly I thought, 'You would miss me horribly, every day. You know how Walter is; he can't tell a good fleece from a bad one; he hates the business and everything to do with it. All he thinks about is playing his lute and making up songs.' I added unkindly, 'And he is delicate, too.'

'I know all that, to my sorrow.'

'Then why do you want to be rid of me? Grandfather, I want to stay here with you and the ponies and the yard...' I began to cry again.

He said, 'But, dear child, in this world we cannot do or have what we want. That is a lesson we must all learn. And we must look to the future. Whether he likes it or not, the business will be Walter's; so will the house. Walter will take himself a wife and where would that leave you? Do you want to be a spinster aunt, unpaid maid to your sister-in-law, unpaid nurse to your brother's children? Maude, a woman needs a husband and a home of her own.'

I said, 'I want this house.' At that he gave a great sigh. 'And what,' I asked, wiping some more tears away with the backs of my hands, 'has going to Beauclaire got to do with whether I have a husband or not? If you provide me with a dowry... You would, wouldn't you?'

'A girl needs more than a dowry. She must be marriageable, Maude. She must know how to run a house, even if she can afford servants; she must be able to sew... and there are other accomplishments.'

'The Devil take accomplishments!' My favourite pack-pony driver, a man called Jack Plant, was always inviting the Devil to take anything which annoyed him.

6

'Now that,' my grandfather said, 'is exactly what your mother says and I have been brought to understand. You have run wild. When she chides you or beats you, you run to me and, because I love you, I am not as firm as I should be. Upon this point I must be firm.' But he looked as though he hated it. Then he said, 'Apart from all else, you have a bad effect upon Walter.'

I said, 'How can you say that? I look after Walter as though he were a baby. At least twice I have saved his life; when the wasp stung his pony and when the ice on the pond gave way. How can you say that I am bad for Walter?' I did not mean to shout but I was shouting again. Also, in rage and astonishment, I had jumped off my grandfather's knee and he, perhaps not knowing what he did, lifted his lame leg and laid it across the other. It seemed to me that perhaps he had been wanting to do that for some time and that I had been in the way.

He said, 'Maude, sit on that stool and I will try to explain. You and Walter are twins; you are—you always have been—bigger and stronger; whatever was to be done you did better, except playing the lute; there you were all thumbs. So the one thing Walter could do better than you could he did, and gave his full attention to. There I do agree with your mother. It is not good for a boy to be overshadowed by his twin sister.'

'Was it good for him to have his life saved? Twice?'

'Maude, everything must be looked at from both sides. When the wasp stung his pony, had you not been there to control it, he might have managed to do so. And the same with the ice on the pond. It cracked, he fell in, you pulled him out. But it would have been better for him to have pulled himself out.'

'He couldn't,' I said. 'But I see how it is. You and Mother have put your heads together and want to be rid of me.'

'You must not say that, Maude. Your mother thinks only that you should have the advantages that she herself had—two years at Beauclaire…'

I knew then that he had failed me and I began the crying that lasted for four days and, as he had said, did no good.

*

7

I knew more about them, my mother and my grandfather, than they knew that I knew. My grandfather, by industry and with luck, had established himself and prospered. He had become moderately rich and built his house, called The Old Vine because it sat on the south-facing slope where formerly grapes had ripened. For my father, Richard Reed, his one living child, he had wanted in every way the best that money could buy. And my father had seen my mother, Anne Blanchefleur, living out at Minsham Old Hall with her crazy old father—once quite a famous knight. Sir Godfrey Blanchefleur had won many tournaments and then, unhorsed, had had to be hammered out of his helm and, having been hurt, had become silly.

So my grandfather had, one might almost say, bought my mother as a bride for his son, my father. A good match or bad, how could I tell? All I knew was that my mother had connections. Lord and Lady Astallon, who had a castle called Beauclaire in Sussex. And there I must go—to be trained and governed, to cease to be a bad influence on Walter and a bone of contention between my mother and my grandfather.

Now they were combined against me and on the day that was fixed I took leave of my home, of my grandfather, of Walter, of my mother—that was easy, since she was the cause of it all—and of all the people, the workers in yard and sheds who had been my friends for as long as I could remember. But I did not cry; four days of tears, four nights of weeping had drained me dry.

I rode my own pony. Brownie. Jack Plant, who had been told to accompany me to a place called Horsham, rode one of the pack ponies, a creature of different breed, slower but capable of bearing more weight. This one carried Jack Plant and a box containing all that my mother thought I should need and that my grandfather could easily afford. She had, she said, gone to Beauclaire with only one pair of shoes; I had four. I had gowns of silk and wool and rolls of stuff to make others when these were outgrown; I had undergarments, headdresses. It was a large box of gear but that pack pony carried it and Jack Plant easily, if slowly, and it was good weather. If every lifted hoof had not taken me one more step from all that I loved and one more step toward what I feared, I should have enjoyed the journey.

The Astallon man, in green livery with a badge on his breast, was ill-tempered before we met him in the inn yard. He said, 'Here I have been for two days, kicking my heels, and the Canterbury pilgrims swarming like fleas.' He rode a tall horse. Jack Plant unfastened my box and put it on the tall horse and said, 'Goodbye. Be happy. We'll miss you sorely.' Then he turned to the Astallon man and said, 'You take good care of our little mistress; she've never been from home afore.'

For me that was another moment of heartbreak— seeing Jack Plant turn, going back to Baildon. I felt quite sick, alone in the world which, judging from the Astallon man's face and manner, was not a friendly place.

The first thing he said as we began our ride together was, 'Is that the best pace you can go?'

I said, 'For a pony of his size Brownie goes fast.'

'We'll see,' he said, and he lifted his whip and brought it down hard on Brownie's rump. Ever since I'd owned him, anyway, the pony had not been struck like that, so he was surprised as well as hurt and broke into his little short-stepped jogging gallop. It did not last long and he settled back to his old steady pace which suited me much better. I was used to riding but not to riding all day, long for days on end, and I was getting sore. The bumping did me no good.

When the Astallon man prepared to hit Brownie again, I shouted, 'Don't do that!' But he did. So next time, just as we were slowing down, I put my hand to my face and let out a yell, 'There's a fly in my eye.'

'Damnation,' he said, coming up beside me. 'Can't you get it out yourself?'

I then snatched the whip from his hand and pulled Brownie around so that my hand, with the whip in it, was as far as possible from the man.

'Give me that whip,' he said between his teeth.

I thought of saying—'Not unless you promise not to hit my

9

pony again.' But the man was not to be trusted, so I said, 'I shan't,' and when he came near enough to reach for it, I brought it down sharply on his wrist.

Mother was always saying that the men in our yard used bad language; she should have heard this man, a lord's servant, with a badge on his breast. I tried to keep Brownie turned and the whip out of reach but of course I was no match for him, a grown man on a tall horse. He took my left arm and began to twist it, very painfully, saying, 'Give me that whip.' The only thing I could do was throw myself out of my saddle. And that surprised him; he was not ready to take my full weight in one hand. I dangled for a second and then he let go and I stood in the road. Still with the whip.

He said, using the most dreadful curses, 'Get back on that pony.' He was in a rather awkward position. He could not put me back on the pony without dismounting himself and I was ready. I had made up my mind that as soon as he began to dismount I would hit his horse, then it would gallop and he would chase it; and I should scramble back on to Brownie and ride off in the other direction—back home.

And all the time, even when I was thinking quite calmly, I was yelling, hoping that somebody would come to my aid. The road was not empty. There were two old women herding along a great gaggle of geese, thirty or forty of them. You'd have thought they would have put in a word for a girl being bullied by a man but they just grinned. There was a man with a donkey with panniers on each side, and he did say,

'Whassa matter?'

'You mind your own business,' the Astallon man said so fiercely that the poor man quailed, said 'Giddup' to his donkey, and passed on.

Then there was a clatter of hooves. A voice cried, 'Make way! Make way!' The Astallon man did edge in toward the side of the road and I held Brownie's bridle and yelled, 'Help! Save me! Help!' I sounded as though I were being murdered.

The first horseman was going too fast. The second stared but rode on; the third rode on, too, and I had time to think—nobody will help me, not old women with geese nor fine gentlemen like these. Then the second one came wheeling around and rode back and said, 'What is all this to-do?'

'Oh, sir, please, help me, help me. Please.'

He was a knight and I knew about knights. My silly old grandfather was one and, though he now had no wits and no sense, he still would not have ridden past and left a girl screaming for help. And his son, my mother's brother, was Sir Godfrey Blanchefleur and though I had only seen him once in my life, I thought he wouldn't have ridden past either.

A remarkable change had come over the Astallon man. He dismounted; he put his hand to his forelock and began to speak in a civil way, pitying himself. Sent, he said, to conduct the little lady and she had no will to go, she would not ride.

'Lies,' I said. 'All lies. I don't want to go to Beauclaire but I was going, until he hit Brownie.'

The knight said, 'If you would not both speak at once, I might make some sense of it.' He leaned forward a little and looked at the horrid man's badge. 'Astallon of Beauclaire?'

'That is so, sir. And sent to conduct...'

'But not to beat my pony,' I said.

'Now, ladies first,' the knight said. 'Tell me why you need help and stand there making a noise like a hound in full cry.'

I told him in as few words as possible. 'You can see I speak the truth,' I said, and I pointed to the two welts on Brownie's smooth rump. 'We were doing our best.'

'As I see. Now let the man speak. Was there any good cause for great speed?'

'I was told to make the best possible speed, sir.'

'But my Lord Astallon would know that a child would not be riding a saddle horse... Is speed of importance? A betrothal? The King visiting Beauclaire? Because if so, I will take this demoiselle, riding pillion, and deliver her. It would be ten miles out of my way but no matter...' He smiled at me. 'If that would suit you,'* he said.

It would have suited me very well. Lifted up out of the dust, taken up upon the splendid horse with this charming knight, who had called me demoiselle instead of girl or wench. But it would mean leaving Brownie with this fellow, bad-tempered to start with—likely, after this, to be worse. So I said:

'Sir knight, that is a most courteous offer but I must refuse it.' I explained why and then said, 'If you would just put the fear of God into him.'

'That I will do.' He looked at my enemy. 'I will ride by way of Beauclaire and I will tell my Lord Astallon that if this pony arrives welted, you have over-driven it and its rider and should yourself be beaten. And I will take that whip.'

I said, 'Oh, thank you. I do thank you. Please, what is your name?'

'My name? Why, what is my name to you?'

'I shall mention it in my prayers every night as long as I live.'

He laughed. 'I shall be much in your debt. My name is John Fitz Arle. What is yours?'

'Maude Reed.'

'I wish you well, and happy. And you, fellow, bear in mind what I said.'

He lifted his hand in salute and rode swiftly away.

Brownie and I settled to our own pace. The man rode in sullen silence and after several days we came to Beauclaire.

CHAPTER II

To me it was an astonishing sight. I had never seen a great lord's establishment before. In and around Baildon the Abbot was the most powerful person, the one who owned most of the land and had the duty of providing twenty knights, mounted and armed, any time the King had need of them. Baildon had its Abbey, very large and solemn, but it was nothing like Beauclaire.

My mother had always spoken of it as a splendid place and had seemed proud of her connection with it but she had not described it in detail, perhaps because to do so was difficult. It stood on a low mound surrounded by a moat and, on the inner side of the moat, by a high stone wall, in parts fallen into ruin. There was the tall, grim castle which, I was to learn, had stood there for more than three hundred years and had once been the place where people lived in time of peace as well as defended in time of war. But castle living can never have been comfortable and so, as time went on, other living quarters had been built, huge houses, tucked in at the foot of the stern tower which was called the Keep.

The houses were of different materials; one block was not unlike my grandfather's house, timber with plaster between the beams; another was all plaster, the colour of a pink rose; another was timber and brick. Their roofs were all at differing levels and some were tiled, some thatched, some of stone. It was, in fact, more like a small town than somebody's house and at the sight of it my heart sank even lower. I was more weary than I had ever been in my life. I was completely homesick, the servant's behaviour had made me miserable; and now I must face a vast number of people, of whom I only knew one, my

13

uncle Sir Godfrey, who was one of Lord Astallon's knights and whom I had seen only once.

The drawbridge over the moat was down and we clattered across through an archway and into a kind of courtyard. I dismounted, very sore and still. From the low, thatched building that made one side of the square some boys, all in green and with badges, came running. One took Brownie and led him away and I thought—there goes my only friend. Another boy shouldered my box and disappeared with it. The horrible servant spoke to me for the first time since our quarrel.

'You go in that door,' he said.

There was a well in the centre of the courtyard; beside it stood a donkey and a little cart made of two shafts, four wheels and an enormous barrel. An old man was drawing water from the well and tipping it into the barrel. The sight and the sound of water made me realise that I was very thirsty; the servant had taken no care for my comfort; it was warm autumn weather and the roads were dusty.

The door toward which the horrid man had jerked his head was inside a deep, dark porch; to walk into it was like going into a den. I could hear, from within the door, a sound of women's voices and laughter. I thought, 'Well, here you go, Maude Reed!' and I made a fist and hammered at the door. Nobody heard or nobody cared. When I had hammered twice, I opened the door. Immediately inside it was a screen, made of wood carved almost as fine as lace, and beyond the screen was a room, the biggest I had ever seen. What was called the solar in my grandfather's house was reckoned the largest and finest room in Baildon but this room was three times its size and half as high again. Yet it seemed full, for all the young ladies in it were wearing dresses with wide, long skirts and headdresses even wider. Four sat together, near one window, stitching away at a piece of embroidery spread over their laps; one sat in the window seat of another window playing a lute, very softly and sweetly. At a table some others were throwing dice and making exclamations. Three stood just inside the screen, talking.

'So I said to her—That is what comes of lending your cloak! For myself I would not lend her a pin.' '

'I would, point first.' They all laughed and I said, 'Please…'

'God have mercy! Where did you spring from?'

'I have come from Baildon. My name is Maude Reed.'

They all looked at me, knowing nothing and not wanting to know. One said,

'Go on, Ella. What did she say to that?' They did what is surely the most hurtful thing in the world. The one who was telling the story went on with it, 'So then she said…' The other two listened, their backs to me. I thought, miserably, that those who were stitching would go on stitching; those who were throwing dice would go on throwing dice. So I went to the one who was playing the lute, planted myself in front of her and said,

'Please, can you help me? My name is Maude Reed. I have been sent here to live. The only person I know is my uncle. Sir Godfrey Blanchefleur, and I have a desperate need to go to the privy.'

I had chosen well. She laid aside the lute and stood up and said, 'Come this way.' She led me into a passage. We went up some steps and down some steps, around another corner, into another passage. There she opened a door and I went into a room where, against a wall, stood a row of great boxes covered in black velvet. She lifted the lid of one and I saw, nested in it, a gleamingly clean copper pot.

'There you are,' she said.

Urgent as my need was, I waited for her to go. I was unused to the ways of the great. At home there was a privy, decently surrounded by bushes, and there we went, one at a time. But here it was different. Even as I hesitated, one of the young women who had been dicing—I knew her by her violet-coloured dress—hurried in, threw up her skirts and took the stool which my friend had opened for me.

'Holy Virgin,' she said. 'That onion broth goes through like a purge.'

Encouraged by her example, I opened the next stool, sat

down and did what I wanted. My friend waited, asking how the dice had fallen.

'Now,' she said to me, 'if anyone knows about you it will be Dame Margaret and she will be in the still-room. Come this way.' She took my hand and smiled at me, and I smiled back at her, and she said, 'Yes, I see. You have the Blanchefleur eyes. Are you homesick?'

'Yes.'

'You'll get over it. You will like living in the Children's Dorter; there are several boys and girls of about your age and Dame Margery is not strict—or so I understand.'

We walked, or so it seemed to me, almost a mile, again turning corners and going up a few stairs and down a few.

'May I ask you your name?'

'Melusine.'

'I have never heard it before.'

'I was named for a fairy lady in a French romance.'

'It is beautiful,' I said, 'it suits you.'

'Ah,' she said, laughing, 'I see you have the Blanchefleur tongue, too.'

'But I mean it.' She was beautiful, with hair so fair, silvery golden, and a pale, unblemished skin and blue eyes; she was more like a fairy than a person; the wired gauze of her headdress could have been the wings of a butterfly. And she was kind and smiling as well. I lost my heart to her; I hoped that Beauclaire would work some magic on me and make me graceful and sweet-spoken. It could never make me fair, of course; my hair was red. But there and then I took her as my model.

We came to a door which she opened and it was like the lid being opened on a spice box. Beyond the door was a room, not large but entirely surrounded by shelves on which stood flasks and bowls and boxes. There was a table and at it stood a stout, elderly woman in a plain linen headdress, moving her hands about in a trough full of some dry-looking, sweet-scented mixture. She looked up and said,

'What have we here?'

'Here we have Maude Reed, Dame Margaret. Come to join the Children's Dorter. She came to the door in the Well Yard.'

'But orders were given. They were told at the main door that she would arrive perhaps today, perhaps tomorrow. Somebody forgot or did not bother. And Dame Margery has taken the children out. Black-berrying. So tomorrow there will be preserves and cordials. And this not yet off my hands. Never mind, never mind. She can stay with me.'

Melusine let go of my hand and smiled and said, 'Good-bye. I hope you will be happy.' And then she was gone.

Dame Margaret said, 'Are you neathanded?' The true answer to that was—No. Neathandedness, needlework, embroidery, and lute playing had never appealed to me and I had resisted all my mother's efforts to make me try harder. What I liked was to heave a bundle of hay, or a measure of corn in a wooden skep, into the mangers of the pack ponies. I liked to do something that tried my strength, used the whole of my body. When the fleeces for which my grandfather had bargained were shorn off, I liked to carry as much as I could lift and put my load on the scales. The fleeces, as they came off the sheep, were dirty, marked with red ochre to show which fleeces he had bought; marked with tar where shepherds had dealt with flyblows; full of thorns, which the sheep had not felt, and full of mud in a wet year.

No, I was not neathanded but now I wished to be.

So I said, 'Yes, Dame Margaret,' and made up my mind to be because I was certain that Melusine was very neathanded.

'Then you can occupy yourself,' Dame Margaret said. She set a number of bowls, some of silver, some of pewter, some of wood, alongside the trough. 'Divide it evenly,' she said, 'but most for the silver.'

Now had my mother, or even my grandfather, ever said such a stupid thing to me I should have stood back on my heels and said, 'What a silly thing to say! To divide evenly and yet to favour one would puzzle God Himself.' That phrase about puzzling God was another I had caught from Jack Plant, like the Devil taking this or that.

17

But here I said nothing. I began taking handfuls of the stuff and very carefully putting it into bowls. It was crumbly and I had to be careful not to spill it. I was being very neathanded. The old woman poured herself half a cupful of some red cordial and sat down to drink it and gossip.

'Reed' she said. 'Was your mother Anne Blanchefleur?'

'Yes.'

'I remember her. A pretty girl but she married a wool merchant.'

I disliked that remark. I was not yet used to the silly grand airs which the servants in great houses gave themselves. I also thought angrily that in our house anyone who arrived after a long journey would have been offered something to eat and drink immediately.

So I said, 'And what is wrong with that? In Baildon my grandfather is well respected and my father was a man of education. He could read and write and play the lute and speak Latin.'

'Maybe,' she said, and I could tell by her voice that she did not believe me. 'But she was a knight's daughter; she should have married a knight, at least. And would have, had she had a penny of dowry.' She looked at me over the rim of the cup. 'I suppose you'll be well provided for in that way.'

I did not answer, not because I was wise but because I was angry. When I had been at Beauclaire a month, I knew that money was regarded as very important; money and land and prospects, which meant that you would have money or land at some time in the future, or that you had some powerful relative who would find you a job at the King's court or in the Church. If I had liked Dame Margaret, I suppose I should have told her that my grandfather owned several sheep runs and was a very prosperous man indeed, that I was his only granddaughter and likely to have quite a large dowry when I married. She would then have told someone else, who would tell another someone, and by the end of the day everyone would have known. As it was, because I did not answer Dame Margaret thought that I kept silence out of shame because I had no dowry. This piece of

18

news was spread about, too, and I never bothered to contradict it.

Just as I was adding the last extra handful to the silver bowls, another white-capped head poked itself around the door and said, 'Dame Margaret, there is neither linen nor towel in the Merlin Chamber and Lord Brede is just arriving.'

'God be my judge!' Dame Margaret exclaimed. 'The Steward told me tomorrow. I swear he said tomorrow.' She went out, flustered.

When the door opened I thought I could smell meat roasting. I thought of supper. I thought of home, of all the bustle and chatter as those of the weavers and drivers and packers who lived on the premises came trooping in. My grandfather, quiet and kindly, would take his place at the table; Mother on his right hand, Walter beside her. My place on his left, empty...

Well, I thought, if nobody cares for me, I must look out for myself. I left the stillroom and set off in search of the place from which the supper scent came. But I was soon lost. I went up a few steps and opened a door and found myself in a room as large as a church, all hung with tapestries. At home we had one, and that was reckoned a marvel, but here they hung edge to edge. Ours was a scene from the Bible—Adam and Eve in the Garden of Eden, Eve offering Adam the fatal apple, the Serpent curled about the tree. Here all the pictures were of knights whose stories I had never heard then. I stared at the brilliant colours and moved on, through another door and into a smaller room whose walls were hung with pink silk. It had a large window and looking out of it I saw, on a lower level and at some distance away, a row of other windows, behind which candles had been lighted. I needed, I told myself, to go down, to hold to the left and to cross a yard. This I did and presently found myself in the dining hall. Supper was over except for a few servants.

I had entered at the lower end. There were several tables; one stood on a little platform at the end farthest from me and looked rather like an altar with a red velvet covering under the white cloth. Another ran down the centre of the hall. The others were simply boards on trestles. I went along the central table, searching for something to eat and, even more important, to drink. There was the litter left from other people's supper, bits of bread and well-gnawed bones and apple cores. The servants looked at me but without curiosity or interest. I found some ale in a jug and drank it; I should have preferred water but the ale quenched my thirst. Then I found a dish with about half a pigeon left in it. I ate that. While I was doing so, a man came along with a bucket into which he swept all the bits; and behind him came a boy with a filthy cloth which he swished across the table. At the Old Vine things were done in better order. Bones were gathered up separately and all soft waste put into the swill pail for the pigs and my mother would never have allowed such a filthy cloth anywhere in the house.

I said to the man with the bucket, 'Can you tell me how to get to the Children's Dorter?'

He gave me some complicated directions which I followed as well as I could, only to find myself at last back in the Well Yard. By this time it was definitely dark and I began to get into a panic. It seemed to me that I should be wandering about, alone and frightened, all through the night; for in the room behind the screen, where I had hoped to find Melusine again, there was nobody at all. Some candles had been lighted there but they were burning low.

This, I thought to myself, is the most hateful place in the world.

Actually all my misery arose from the fact that I had been sent to the wrong door. Muddled as this household seemed to be, everybody in it had his or her place, his or her duties. I had missed my place; it was nobody's duty to look after me. I honestly believe that in a place like Beauclaire, so long as you were decently dressed and bothered nobody, you could live unnoticed for a week or longer.

However, at last I heard music and the sound of someone singing. Guided by this, I opened yet another door and found myself back in the room hung with tapestries. It was, I soon learned, called the Long Gallery. It was full of people, all with their backs to me; some of the ladies sat on stools, benches or chairs, with gentlemen standing around. They were all listening to the music which came from the far end of the room.

I went in like a lost pup in search of a master. I thought I might recognise my Uncle Godfrey again; I knew I should recognise Melusine. Again nobody asked me who I was or what I was doing there. I pushed along until I could see the musicians; a man with a lute, a man with a harp, a boy with a wooden frame from which hung a number of little bells.

Then, out of a group of people, Melusine moved forward just as the lute player swept his fingers over the strings on the last note of the song.

'You again!' she said. 'You should be abed.'

'I've been lost. Dame Margaret...' I began.

'Never mind that now. Come and make your duty '

Holding me by the hand, she led me toward a lady who sat on a bench with high, inturned ends, all gilded. She looked more like a statue than a woman, partly because the colour on her face was all laid on and her eyebrows had been shaved off and painted on again, at least an inch higher; her dress was cloth of gold and her hair was held in a gold net.

Melusine let go my hand and said, rather stiffly, 'Madame, this is Maude Reed.'

My mother had taught me to curtsy and to Lady Astallon I made one of my very best. Rising out of it I could see that my name meant nothing to her but she said, 'You are welcome.'

'My mother,' I said, 'sent her loving greetings and her gratitude for taking me into your household.'

The faint look of surprise which her eyebrows gave her did not change. Somebody leaned over her shoulder and murmured in her ear. Then she knew who I was.

'Ah yes, Sir Godfrey's niece. You will join the Dorter and, I hope, learn well.' She then dismissed me from her presence and from her mind. She said, 'Let the harpist have his turn.'

Melusine said, 'Come, I will take you to Dame Margery.'

We were almost out of the room and most attention was turned to the harpist, who had begun to play, when a gentleman

21

came to Melusine's side, walked a step or two with us and said, in a quiet and rather nasty voice,

'You waste your time. Lady Melusine. Godfrey is not to be reached that way. And my offer is still good.'

'But not to me,' she said. I should not have thought that she could have used so sharp a tone, even to one who spoke nastily.

It was another long walk but at last we halted outside a door. Melusine said, 'Here we are. Our paths may not cross again for many a long day but I hope you will be happy.' She kissed me, a kiss that was like a brush from a butterfly's wing. Then she opened the door and said, 'Dame Margery, this is Maude Reed.'

CHAPTER III

The Children's Dorter at Beauclaire, as in many similar places, was an establishment on its own. It consisted of three large rooms and two small ones, all on the top floor of the pink-plastered house. There was a sleeping chamber for girls and another for boys, the big living room where we took our meals, except midday dinner, Dame Margery's own little bedchamber and another little room into which we were banished if we were sick—or naughty.

There were eight of us. First and foremost the children of the house, my very distant cousins: Constance, who was eight, and Ralph, who was six and who would, in due time, be sent to serve as page to another great household—possibly even a royal one, like Westminster, Windsor. There were two boys aged ten and seven, Henry and William Rancon. In the French wars, lately ended, their father had been killed and Lord Astallon was doing his duty by them, their father having been one of his knights. There was a girl exactly my age, Helen Beaufort, a daughter born out of wedlock to the great Cardinal Beaufort, and there was another girl, rather older, Madge Fitz-Herbert, who was an orphan. She was Lord Astallon's ward—a term I did not understand until it was explained to me. Then I understood.

A girl who had no father and no brother and so was going to inherit money and land was what was called an heiress and had to be looked after and guarded. Before they went to war or even to fight in an ordinary tournament, careful men arranged that should they die and leave a female child, some other man should take charge of her until she married. And even I, hating it all, this talk about dowries, could see that Madge Fitz-Herbert did need a guardian to protect her because she was

23

simpleminded. You had only to look at her to see that if she had been born poor she would have been the town idiot. But, it was said, you could get on to a good, sturdy, active horse and ride for two days and that horse would never once set foot on ground that did not belong to Madge Fitz-Herbert, who was now thirteen. The eighth member of this community was a girl, Alison Fortescue, about my own age and, like me, distantly related to the Astallon family.

On the whole, it was a happy life. Dame Margery, though she was growing old, was fond of the out-of-doors and liked walking, so most days we went out into the woods or the great open fields of the manor. We gathered anything that was in season—blackberries, mushrooms, hazelnuts, tiny wild strawberries, any flower that happened to be in bloom and certain plants which Dame Margery believed to be good for our health.

The boys, of course, were much freer than we girls were. There was not much that they could be expected to learn from Dame Margery and they were only in the Children's Dorter until such time as they were old enough to be pages and then squires; their hard part was still to come. But although they were free while we sewed and did embroidery and learned to spin, both wool and flax, they, like us, must learn to be mannerly and—almost the most important thing of all—to be self-controlled. Under Dame Margery's eye you could say the most horrid, most hurtful things, so long as you said them civilly. When the boys quarrelled, as they often did. Dame Margery said, 'Out into the yard and settle it,' and the loser never had any sympathy. 'That may teach you not to pick quarrels,' she would say, or, 'You will bear harder knocks, if you live.' Once when I said something was unfair, she said to me, 'And what led you to expect that things should be fair? Permit me to point out that you are living in the world, not in Paradise.'

'Permit me to point out' or 'Allow me to say' were phrases we must all use in order to seem civil. Having said that, so long as you did not yell, you were permitted to say almost anything. 'Allow me to say that you are a liar,' or 'Permit me to point out that you eat like a pig,' might make the other person angry but did not bring any punishment from Dame Margery.

We all, boys and girls alike, had to practice standing, very upright and without fidgeting, for what seemed endless hours.

'When you are page or squire to some great lord, or when you wait upon some great lady, you will stand,' Dame Margery said. 'I want nobody to say that I brought you up to be soft.' The punishment for fidgeting was to stand, for double the time, with your hands clasped on the top of your head.

It seemed to be taken for granted that we should all go on living in Beauclaire or someplace very much like it. But I still dreamed of my grandfather's house and my grandfather's business. He was old, he was lame, Walter would never settle down to the business; so who would be left, except me? In two years' time I should not be some great lady's waiting woman. I should, I was almost certain, be back in Baildon and perhaps saying to some shepherd who had not done his duty, 'Permit me to say that you are a cheating rogue!' That was a funny thought and I grinned to myself as I thought it. And then I saw something; not very clearly, just a glimmer, no more. Civility had uses. 'Permit me to point out that you are a cheating rogue!' did carry more weight than 'You cheating rogue!' I was going to be a wool merchant but I was going to be such a wool merchant as the world had not yet seen. A woman wool merchant and a very grand one. 'Allow me to say... never in my life have I seen such rotten fleeces.' That would astonish them!

At Beauclaire there were two gardens; we were allowed only into the one called the Low Garden. It was old. Dame Margery was fond of pointing out to us how lucky we were to live in such settled times, able to walk where we would. Once upon a time, she said, it was only safe for people to exercise their legs and take the air in the Low Garden which was inside the castle walls. Now there was a much bigger one on the other side of the moat but grown-up people, taking their pleasure there, did not wish to be disturbed by children playing. So the Low Garden was for us.

One bright spring day, when I had been at Beauclaire for five months the boys, led by Henry Rancon, as always, found a new game. Part of the wall of the Low Garden was, as the castle wall was in various places, broken down and part was firm and solid. They scrambled up the broken part and walked about the sound part, strutting like cockerels and jeering at us, saying that they were doing what no girl could do.

'I bet I can,' I said. In a way I was prepared to give way to Henry Rancon who, though younger than I, was very bold and active. He was soon to have his eleventh birthday and become a page when, as Dame Margery often warned him, he would go through the mill. But the idea that William and Ralph, simply because they were boys, could do what I could not, made me angry.

I scrambled up the ruined part of the wall and stood on the top of the sound part. It was about twelve inches wide and there was no good reason why anybody shouldn't walk up and down, up and down forever. Walking on a flat floor you don't take up more than twelve inches. But I made the mistake of looking down. On my left, the wall dropped about ten feet, straight into the moat; on my right, about ten feet into the garden. I had a horrible feeling; my stomach dropped, my eyes blurred, my head began to spin, my knees went weak. I tried to remember all that Dame Margery had said about self-control, the mastery of self. I managed perhaps ten steps, to where that stretch of wall ended in a little tower. I reached it and put my back against it and felt safe, in a silly way. Silly because I knew I could not stay there forever; I must take those ten steps back. And I knew I could not. Allow me to say, Maude Reed, that you have taken on something no girl should do. Fear and desperation made me reckless. I said, 'I'll wager none of you can do this!' I turned toward the garden and jumped. A sickening pain stabbed through my ankle as I landed badly but Dame Margery's training was already beginning to tell. I gave no sign of distress. I stood up, straight and still, and looked Henry Rancon straight in the eye. 'Let me see you do it,' I said.

He walked up the bit of ruined wall, took the necessary paces, turned, and jumped; a perfect landing. Ralph Astallon

said, 'I cannot jump, it would jar the tooth that is troubling me.'
William Rancon said, 'I will do it another day.'

Whether my ankle was broken or merely sprained I never
knew. I said nothing about it; it hurt worse than a toothache but
I would not even allow myself to hobble. It swelled and then
went back to its ordinary size. But for years it hurt if I ran or
took an exceptionally heavy step and it always hurt just before
rain.

However, that piece of recklessness gained me more than it
lost me, for after that Henry Rancon favoured me with a gruff,
offhand kind of friendship. I was, in fact, better company for
him than either his brother or Ralph but up to that day he had, I
think, been rather ashamed to include me in their games. Now
he always did; and best of all, it was through him that I got back
my pony, Brownie.

I had seen the pony almost every day, once I had found my
way to the stables; I took him apples and bread crusts. And,
since my grandfather had given me plenty of pocket money, I
had been able to bribe one of the stable boys to exercise him
a little and to give him a brush down occasionally. But I had
not been able to ride him because none of the other girls rode
and Dame Margery refused to allow me to go riding alone. The
boys, of course, rode when and where they liked.

All Henry's games were concerned with playing at being a
knight. It was his one ambition. He knew he still had a long
way to go; he must be a page first, either in this house or one
like it; then he would be a knight's squire, tending his horse and
looking after his armour; and then, if he was brave enough and
strong enough and lucky enough, he would be knighted himself
and become Sir Henry Rancon.

In the games they had played before I was allowed to join
in, Henry had always been a knight and so had Ralph because,
though he was the younger, he was the son of the house; and
William had had to pretend to be squire to them both which
gave him rather a hard time of it. Now I was Henry's squire and
one day he said to me, 'Reed, it is a pity that you do not ride.
To have a squire unmounted is a great handicap to a knight.'

I replied in the proper manner. 'Sir,' I said, 'I can ride and I have a steed in the stables.'

Henry thought I was pretending and said, 'That, Reed, is carrying things too far.'

I said, 'Sir, may I show you my horse?'

Still doubting, he came with me to the stable where my good little pony greeted me in a way that left no doubt about whose pony he was.

'My boy,' Henry said to me, giving me such a hearty thump on the back that I almost fell over, 'this is wonderful. Now we can joust!' Jousting was the kind of mock warfare by which knights kept in practice.

However, we had reckoned without Dame Margery. Naturally we did not mention jousting, we simply asked permission for me to ride with the boys and she pointed out that my time would be better spent on more feminine occupations. But she was good-natured at heart and tried to get out of it by saying that she thought my mother should be asked; one day she would ask the Lady Melusine, who could write, to write a letter to my mother to find out her wishes.

'But Dame Margery, that would take weeks,' I said. Then I had a very good idea. 'My uncle is here,' I said. 'He would know my mother's wishes on any matter concerning me.'

My Uncle Godfrey had not been at Beauclaire when I arrived. He had been at a tournament in Winchester and had come back with a silver cup, full of gold pieces. My Lord Astallon was pleased with him because this success reflected glory upon Beauclaire.

Since his return I had seen him several times in the dining hall and once to speak to. He said I had grown since he saw me last—and indeed it would have been strange if I had not. He said he hoped I was enjoying myself at Beauclaire. But he said that in such a way that I knew he did not care whether I was happy or not. I guessed that if asked whether my mother wished me to ride he'd say what came easiest which would be Yes. He was like that. However, he did better than that; he pointed out to Dame Margery that I should one day be going back to Baildon where, if I could not ride, I should be extremely lonely, unable to make visits because the Old Vine was not the kind of house where there was always a servant to spare to take a female riding pillion. He added that my mother herself rode.

So after that I was allowed to ride with the boys—not always, but often enough. We went to a little clearing in the woods where Henry had rigged up copies of the things real knights used on the real practice ground. There was a ring swinging from a pole. We took long sticks in our hands—they were our lances—and rode at this ring as fast as we could make our ponies go, the idea being to get the stick through the ring. Then, between two posts, there was a sack stuffed with straw. That was a man and he had to be stabbed. We had no swords, of course, but we had what was almost as dangerous, knives tied on to sticks.

I took to these, and other such games, as a duck takes to water and was soon so much better than either William or Ralph that the scores became very lopsided. Sir Ralph and his squire were no match for Henry and his, so one day Henry decided to knight me so that we could compete with one another. In his game Henry had been obliged to knight himself but for me he made a ceremony of it. He was the King. (The King's name was Henry at that time.) I had to kneel and put both my hands between his and swear to be his liege man and serve him in life and limb and he struck me on the shoulder with his 'sword' and said, 'Arise, Sir Reed.' Before this ceremony, Henry explained, I should have taken a bath and spent a night awake and praying in a church but under Dame Margery's eye this was impossible, so I was 'knighted on the field,' as did sometimes happen after a battle in which a man had shown himself to be very brave.

Then there was a squabble. William said, 'Now there are three knights and only one squire. I want to be a knight, too.' So Henry knighted him and after that we all had imaginary squires to whom we gave orders and then did the work ourselves. I called mine John because of the man who had been my friend on the road and for whom I did pray every night, though I was rapidly forgetting what he looked like. After that the games were more even, with Sir Henry and Sir Ralph playing against Sir Reed and Sir William, and despite some bumps and bruises and scratches about which, like brave and honourable knights, we made no fuss, we had wonderful times.

I sometimes think, looking back, that there is no time so happy as that part of childhood where one lives in a world of make-believe. Even our imaginary squires seemed real to us, until we had jogged back, stabled our fiery steeds and climbed the stairs to the Children's Dorter, where Dame Margery, not without reason, made us wash our hands before dinner.

CHAPTER IV

Christmas brought another change.

I had presents from home—a cloak from my mother, a gold-and-pearl pin from my grandfather and a square of parchment with writing on it. All down the left-hand side of it there were leaves and berries, painted in their proper colours, and some of the letters in the writing were coloured, too.

'I know what it is,' Dame Margery said when I showed it to her. 'It is a Christmas Piece. You must ask the Lady Melusine to read it to you.'

'May I do so now, please?'

I had seen Melusine as I had seen my uncle—across the dining hall. Between the ladies and the children at Beauclaire there was a great gulf fixed. Ladies' chatter was regarded as unfit for children's ears and ladies did not want children underfoot. But now I had permission to go to the Well Yard Room and I went eagerly.

'Yes, it is a Christmas Piece, to bring you good wishes,' Melusine said when she had studied it. She read out what it said.

'On this, the Birthday of Our Blessed Lord, I send Greetings to my Dear Sister and wish you joy and God's Blessing on you, from your Brother Walter Reed.'

'Would you be so kind as to read it again?' I asked. She read it in all three times. By then I had it pat, having a sharp memory.

Melusine said, 'He must be a clever scholar. It is well written and very even. Who is his teacher?'

'I do not know. There was talk, when I left, of his going to the monks' school in Baildon but sometimes my mother and

31

grandfather thought him not strong enough and then there was talk of his having a tutor.'

'He is well taught,' she said. 'And you, Maude; how are you getting on?'

She was so kind and so pretty, I felt that I could have told her all about the games with me being Sir Reed. But something warned me. For one thing, they were secret; for another thing, to speak of them would make them seem less real; and for yet another thing—well, they were not of her world. I was aware of a pull. There was the world of women, pretty, soft, sweetly scented; and the world of men, harsh and tough. I was like a person sitting astride a gate, half here, half there.

And then I realised that there was yet another world, neither male nor female—the world of reading and writing. And there was Melusine, also like a person sitting astride a gate, on one side of her the world ruled by the needle and curtsies and chatter and headdresses, on the other the world of pens and the words they wrote.

Out of all this I brought one sentence. I said, 'I wish I could read and write.'

She said, 'I would most gladly teach you, Maude, if time and opportunity could be found.'

'Would you?' She nodded, and I said, 'I will make the time and the opportunity.'

I thought of my Uncle Godfrey. Over the matter of riding he had stood by me, knowing what my life was to be. Perhaps over this, too, he would be helpful. And he was.

'Who would teach you, Maude?'

'The Lady Melusine.'

'So!' he said. 'Then I will speak for you to my Lady Astallon.'

He was as good as his word. But then one of those ridiculous situations, typical of Beauclaire where waste and sparingness ran side by side, cropped up.

There came a day when Dame Margery said, 'Maude wishes to have lessons in reading and writing but my Lady thinks it would be a waste of time for the Lady Melusine to have only one pupil. Does any one of you wish to have lessons?'

The silence was so silent that it rang.

Next morning Sir Henry and Sir Reed, Sir Ralph and Sir William, followed by their invisible squires, rode out to the clearing in the woods. And as we rode I said, 'Sir Henry, I swore to be your liege man.'

'Yes; and nobody ever had a better.'

'The liege lord owes a duty to his liege man. Is that not so. Sir Henry?'

'A liege and his lord are one,' he said.

'When it suits,' I said. 'Yesterday you were not one with me. When Dame Margery asked if anyone else wanted to take lessons, you stayed silent. You failed me as badly as Oliver failed Roland at Roncevalles.'

I was using his own words against him. He it was who had taken me around the Long Gallery and told me the story of Saint George and the Dragon, of Roland and Oliver and the horn.

Rebuke always made him sulky and we rode in silence for a long time. Then he said, with a kind of violence, 'All right then, I'll say I wish to take lessons. That is a lie and I will confess it and do my penance...' The Chaplain at Beauclaire was strict and dealt out penances pretty freely and a lie was a lie. I could see Henry kneeling on cold stone and saying maybe as many as ten Paternosters... 'Our Father that art in Heaven...' right through.

I said, 'I don't want to get you into trouble, Henry. Could you not persuade yourself that you do wish to read and write? Then there would be no lie and no penance.'

He said, 'Writing is for churchmen or scribes. I have no taste and no need for it. But you are my man and I your lord and for that reason I will do it.'

Dame Margery almost dropped dead from surprise when Henry Rancon said he wished to take lessons. But she ran away and reported and soon after Christmas, which was very gay and rowdy, the lessons were arranged in a funny dark little room—all that could be spared in this vast house—three days a week, immediately after dinner. And Henry's self-sacrifice was not wasted, for almost as soon as we had settled down, with ink and quill and parchment, along came my Uncle Godfrey, graceful, lounging, smiling and saying that he wished to take lessons too.

He also should have done penance for lying. He had no wish to learn, and why should he? The man who had carried off the silver cup at Winchester had no need to learn the alphabet and how to put letters together to make words. He and Henry would go off into the corner and carry on the make-believe game, dealing blows, laughing, while Melusine taught me. Presently she would say, 'Enough for today.' She would say to me, 'You will make a good scholar,' and my uncle would say to Henry, 'You have all the makings of a knight.' And then, well pleased, Henry and I would run off together.

So the year grew; every day had a little more daylight and soon it was Easter and Henry had his eleventh birthday and went to be a page. I knew I should miss our games but he was so happy to be making this step out of childhood to manhood that I said nothing to sadden him. After that I saw him, now wearing the Astallon green and badge, only in the dining hall.

But of course I was growing older too and I now had my lessons to interest me. I was very proud when I could copy some words which Melusine had written out for me, a greeting to Walter. That, I thought, would surprise him.

My Uncle Godfrey continued to come to the little room where I had lessons, generally with some joke—'I must see how my niece is getting on,' he would say; or 'I must make sure that you are not wasting your time, my Lady Melusine.' Once she answered rather sharply and said, 'It is you who waste my time, Sir Godfrey.' And he said, 'Oh, no. Never think that.'

Toward the middle of May he went away again, making a round of the tournaments. After that I had Melusine to myself and I was glad. With me he was out of sight, out of mind but always, sooner or later, she would mention him, saying that they had had fine weather for the Dover Tournament or that she hoped he was doing well at Windsor. From this I gathered that she was in love with him. And by this time, thanks to

Helen Beaufort and Alison Fortescue, I knew all about being in love.

Being in love was a kind of game that men and women played at, rather as the boys and I had played at being knights. It had nothing at all to do with marriage; marriages were arranged by parents or guardians, often by the King himself. In fact, both Helen and Alison had husbands already chosen for them and they were not looking forward to marriage at all. What they were looking forward to was being old enough to play at this love game.

So the question I asked one afternoon when Melusine mentioned my uncle was a very natural one. I said, 'Does he carry your colour?' For that was what a knight in love did; he took something belonging to his lady, a knot of ribbon or lace or even a glove and fixed it to his helmet. And if he happened to win a trophy he would offer it to the lady who would pretend to take it and smile and then give it back.

When I asked my question, Melusine, whose cheeks were never much brighter than a hedge rose, blushed scarlet.

'No; like every other Astallon knight, he wears my Lady's knot of gold ribbon. But I also gave him a token and that he wears next to his heart. In any case he could not wear it openly because we are not betrothed and I am not married.'

'I do not understand that,' I said. There was evidently more to this game of being in love than Helen or Alison knew.

'A lady who is betrothed to a man may give him a favour. A lady who is married—like my Lady Astallon—may give a dozen men favours. But for Sir Godfrey to wear my favour would cause talk of a scandalous kind.'

That I did not understand either, but perhaps I might learn.

'Why do you and my uncle not become betrothed?'

'There are reasons.'

'Are you promised to someone else?'

'No. I have no dowry.'

'Is he promised?'

'No. He has no money.'

I said, 'I can get you a dowry. You can have mine! My

grandfather is not much thought of here, but he is rich and very generous. I have no mind to get married, so what he would give to me he can give to you. After all, when you are married you will be part of the family.'

She laughed. 'My sweet innocent, that is not the way things are done, but I thank you for the thought.' She looked at me, half teasing, and said, 'What makes you think you will not marry?'

'Promise not to laugh. Very well. I mean to be a wool merchant. And then, you see, it would not do for me to be married. My husband might not know the trade and that would lead to arguments. And be bad for the business.'

Despite her promise she did laugh. 'You are the quaintest girl. Wait two years and you will be laughing at yourself.'

'But I mean it. When I have done my time here to my mother's satisfaction I shall go back to Baildon and work with my grandfather until I know everything and then I shall be a wool merchant.'

'But you have a brother. What about him?'

'He hates the business. So I shall run it. I shall give him most of the money, I shall keep just enough to be grand. And I shall keep the house. When he marries he can build himself a new one.'

'Well,' she said, 'it is a curious dream. But they sometimes come true. What is Minsham Old Hall like?'

'Horrible,' I said, taken by surprise by the sudden question.

'In what way?'

'Cold and draughty and bare, like a barn. My grandfather Blanchefleur cannot afford to mend the roof. He had one wall hanging once, and even that he was forced to sell to my other grandfather.'

'You do depress me,' she said, but she sounded quite gay. 'Mended up and properly furnished, it would be a place to live in. You see, Maude... I will tell you something but it is a most secret secret. Swear not to tell...'

'On the Cross of Our Blessed Lord.'

'Well, one day, when... when things go right, your uncle and

I are going to marry and live at Minsham Old Hall. He hopes to get into the service of the Abbot of Baildon.'

I said, 'That is the most wonderful news. You will be my aunt and my neighbour. One of our sheepruns is at Minsham. I shall have an excuse to ride that way often. Thank you for telling me, Melusine. You have made me very happy. The one thing I dreaded about leaving Beauclaire was the thought of never seeing you again.'

She gave me one of those butterfly kisses and said, 'Run along. And remember not to talk in your sleep. Or out of it.'

I thought she has no dowry and he has no money, except when gold pieces are the prize, which was not often. And being one of the Abbot's knights would not bring in much. I planned wild acts of generosity— seeing myself as a rich wool merchant. I'd have the roof mended for her; I'd put hangings on those bare walls and meat in the larder. When I thought like that, I completely forgot that I was only twelve and had a long, hard apprenticeship to the trade still to do; that my grandfather must be talked around and my mother shouted down... Oh no, not shouted, at Beauclaire one learned not to shout... argued down, with the soft, sour-sweet manner which ladies were allowed to use. Of this I will give one example.

Helen Beaufort was very proud of her high connections and one day said something taunting about my father, the wool merchant. I said to her, 'My father may have been a wool merchant. But he married my mother and when I was born did not pretend I was his niece.' Now for that I should have been soundly smacked; it was an unpardonable thing to say. But Dame Margery, who had overheard it all, said, 'Good, I am glad to see that you are learning to defend yourself without shouts and blows.'

I had learned and was still learning and I could imagine myself saying quietly to my mother, 'And who will keep this good business going and provide you with the comforts you so much love if I do not? Walter could not run the Old Vine for a week.'

I should win. I knew it in my heart. And I went on planning as though victory were already certain.

CHAPTER V

That was such a fair bright summer, almost as if God knew... In Suffolk I have heard shepherds and farmers speak of a lovely day as 'a weather breeder,' meaning that rough weather was on its way.

In fact, though we did not then know it, all over England a fearful storm was brewing up. It had a pretty name—it was called the War of the Roses because the Lancastrians took a red rose for their badge and the Yorkists chose white. But it was, for all its pleasant name, a horrible war and it put an end to such places as Beauclaire and to such people as my Lord Astallon who, on his own land and in his own house, had been almost a king. I lived to see the war end and a man called Henry Tudor on the throne and one of the first laws he passed was that nobody, however great, might dress his servants in uniform or give them badges.

Sometimes I wonder about my distant cousin, Lord Astallon, and ask myself whether he saw what was coming and was determined not to take sides or to join any party. Certainly he refused to go to London or to appear at Court, though he had, I was told, a large house in the Strand. My Lady Astallon would have loved to go to London and show off her beauty and her clothes and her jewels; but he would not budge and when the annual housecleaning time came around, the Beauclaire household simply went a mere ten miles to a manor house called Sumhurst.

The housecleaning move was new to me because I had always lived in a house small enough to deal with its own waste week by week. But with so many people living together, the cesspools and the drains could not deal with it all. Even the King must move from palace to palace.

Beauclaire went to Sumhurst, which was small. The knights were already away. Some of the waiting ladies went home to visit their families. Some of the men-at-arms went home to their families to help fetch in the hay and then the corn. But even so, Sumhurst was too small to house all the Beauclaire household and we of the Children's Dorter were left behind.

We had a splendid time. We were a little like the remnants of an army, given the run of enemy territory. We played battledore and shuttlecock in the Long Gallery and hide-and-seek all over the house. Dame Margery took us out—the girls well protected from freckles and sunburn by great sunbonnets—into the hay and then the harvest fields. On the day when the moat was dredged the stench was so horrid that no amount of moving about inside the house could avoid it, so we took our food out and cooked it over a fire of sticks. The meat was burned black on the outside and red-raw within but it tasted better than such spoiled meat would have done indoors.

While we enjoyed this unusual freedom, servants beat beds and bleached linen and polished floors and panels with beeswax. And then it was September.

Into the sweetened, clean-smelling house, they came trooping back.

Fashion I never understood and never shall. My Lady Astallon still wore on her golden hair her golden net. She had not changed; it was as though she said, 'This is for me, let the rest do as they wish.' And I noted that; I thought that when I was a wool merchant I would find some form of dress suitable to me and to my purpose and hold to it. But curiously enough, every other lady had changed. The pretty, wide, butterfly-winged headdress was nowhere to be seen. The headdresses were higher and narrower, not unlike a church steeple, and the veils no longer fell softly to each side but down at the back, like the loose part of a peasant's hood.

Melusine looked beautiful in hers but she would have looked beautiful in anything.

I was, of course, looking at the reassembled household in the dining hall. It was September again a year almost to the day since I had arrived here, at the wrong door. Having found Melusine, my eye sought Henry Rancon, once my liege lord, once my fellow knight.

Surely nobody had ever grown so much in three months. And was I the only person to notice that he had outgrown his clothes, trunks and tunic barely meeting, tunic strained across the shoulders, sleeves three inches short. I had a horrid thought. I thought—for him it will always be that way, never enough because he has no parents and his ambition, like mine, is a burden. In my mind I shouldered him, too. I thought to myself, 'When I am a wool merchant, I will buy him a great horse, the kind called destrier; I will give him a sword forged in Toledo— Spanish steel was the best in the world—and he shall have clothes, silk, velvet, fine linen, because he is my friend '

Dreaming my dreams, I went back to the Children's Dorter, now back in place but changed. It had always centred around my distant cousins, Constance and Ralph, and around the thought that a woman who could look after two children could with equal ease look after eight or nine. We had all aged by a year and there were differences. We were allowed to move, step by step, out of the narrow rut along which we had run into the wider, grown-up world.

In this autumn, no new inmate for the Children's Dorter had arrived; I do not know for what reason, unless it was that Dame Margery was growing old and talked more and more of the day when she would have done with us and go to live out the rest of her life in a nunnery. Not a nun. 'Oh no,' she said, 'I have no vocation and I am too old. To offer God the dregs of one's life, that would be insulting. But I can still see, God be praised, and I can sew, make and mend. At Crowhurst there will be a place for me and there I shall end my days in peace and quiet. And without trouble.'

When she said this she looked at poor Madge Fitz-Herbert, surely the least troublesome of us all. She seldom spoke, even, and when she did, it was as though her mouth were full of flannel. She was obedient, like a dog or a donkey. It took her about ten minutes to thread a needle. Often I did it for her

40

but once it was threaded she would stitch away, very slowly, very clumsily, but patiently. She never quarrelled or uttered a complaint. I could not see why, when Dame Margery spoke of trouble, she should so often look at poor Madge.

Between the return to the purified house and the coming of winter with its mud and its snow, Beauclaire made merry and this year we were allowed to do some things which last year had been forbidden.

Once, when there were some visiting knights, we watched a tournament. It was very exciting. The tourney ground lay beyond the moat, on the south side. It was a vast oblong surrounded by wooden stands over which various kinds of cloth could be hung. There was space behind the hangings at each end for knights and their horses and their squires and their pages; room for smiths who would shoe a horse or mend a piece of armour and for barber-surgeons who would set a broken limb or stop a wound from bleeding. On a third side there was a gallery, high from the ground and always hung with silk and velvet and cloth of gold; it was like a room on stilts. In the centre was the part called the Ladies' Gallery; it was furnished with benches and had an awning. Into this we were allowed on condition that we did not make nuisances of ourselves.

In a tournament the idea was for two knights to ride at one another and each try to unhorse the other. What weapon should be used was decided beforehand—lances, maces or swords. Tournament swords had no points and their edges were blunted—not half as dangerous as our knives tied to sticks; but then we had never ridden at one another with them, only at the sack. Under their gaily-coloured mantles the knights wore armour which was heavy; their helmets were heavy, too, so when a knight was unhorsed he fell with a great thud.

Generally it was one man against one man but often, at the end, there would be a cry, 'Astallon against Bedford!' or 'Astallon against all!' Then six or eight knights would line up at each end and charge. The din and the dust then were dreadful. I have seen four knights unhorsed in a single melée but the only bad accident I ever witnessed was when a visiting knight was unhorsed and his own horse stepped on him. It must have been only a half-trained horse to do such a thing. When they were fully trained, chargers could pick their way over a battlefield strewn with men and never step on one.

In that autumn, too, we were allowed into the Long Gallery, once to watch some mummers, who were very funny indeed, and once to join in the dancing. The dancing was another time when Dame Margery looked at Madge and sighed and spoke of trouble. 'I have done my best,' she said, 'but no woman can put in what God left out.' And the truth was that no teacher on earth could have made Madge dance. For one thing she could not count. Two to the left, two to the right simply meant nothing to her.

I understood a little—but far from all—of what was going on when one evening Dame Margaret lumbered up with a jug of the new blackberry cordial which she wanted Dame Margery to sample. We had gathered the blackberries but were not offered so much as a sip. They went into Dame Margery's little room but they did not close the door. Alison and I were playing checkers with a beautiful set that had been one of her birthday presents. The others were playing blind man's buff which even Madge could play. In fact, now that I come to think of it, it was the only game at which she was any good at all. With her eyes blinded with a cloth, she was no more clumsy and awkward than at other times.

I was waiting for Alison to make her next move—and I was ready for it. I'd led her into a trap; she would take the invitation and then I should pounce—when I heard Dame Margery say,

'I truly thought another year, maybe two. The Lady Constance is nine. I gave myself at least another year. But everything is so hurried these days. Another year and we should surely be rid of that poor thing. Then I could have shown my work with pride. Even the wool merchant's daughter can skip and turn and make a square or a chain with the best.'

Oh, I thought. Thank you, Dame Margery!

Dame Margaret said, 'You take it too hard. One failure,

among so many. I have had failures too. I threw them away and
said nothing.'

'I can hardly throw Madge Fitz-Herbert away, Dame
Margaret. But to produce her will shame me. She is fourteen
and for all she knows could have arrived here yesterday. But
can any woman put in what God left out?'

'You said that before,' Dame Margaret said. 'It is a thing
old women should be aware of, saying the same thing over
and over. Put a fine headdress on her and who will notice? It
was a thing I learned long long ago, in my Lord Bowdegrave's
kitchen at Abhurst. Put enough sauce on it, even on stinking
fish or the last bit of beef out of the salt barrel, and it serves.'

Alison made the move that I had foreseen, took away my
piece and left herself open. I moved my piece, lurking and sly,
one, two three. The game was as good as over and I could give
my thoughts to headdresses.

There was something special about headdresses. They were
a sign of rank. We children had hitherto worn our own hair
in the house. Outside, in winter we wore woollen caps and in
summer sunbonnets. But we must now be fitted out in order to
dance, to be presentable, as Dame Margery said. She had noted
the new fashion.

When we trooped down to the Long Gallery we all wore
stiffened cones on our heads with veils floating backward. I
wore my grandfather's Christmas gift, the pearl-and-gold pin,
to hold my veil to the top of my steeple. Helen and Alison
were just as well equipped but Madge—to look at her made
you blink. All across the edge of her steeple-shaped cone was
a great broad band made partly of diamonds and partly of glass
beads so like diamonds that you had to look very closely to tell
one from the other. The diamonds caught the candlelight and
broke it up into all the colours of the rainbow. Then the beads
took up whichever colour was nearest—red, blue, yellow,
purple—and gave it back. 'Put a fine headdress on her and who
will notice?' Who will even see, blinded by such brilliance, the
dull, blank, idiot stare or count the miscounted steps, the left
hand held out when the right should have been?

43

Between the dances we drank wine, cooled from having been hung down the well all day. And we ate little honey cakes, and sausages skinned and sliced small, and the dark dried plums from France called prunes and—rarest treat of all—little pieces of ginger, at once stinging and succulent, a pain and a delight.

The tourneys and the dancing I remember with pleasure. And then, just before all the visitors went home and Beauclaire settled down for the winter, there came something which I remember with horror—a bear-baiting.

Perhaps it was not ill meant. All around there were the fields, now cleared of the harvest, and the peasants deserved some entertainment. Tournaments and dancing in the Long Gallery were not for them but a bear-baiting they could not only watch but share since, if they wished, they could bring their own dogs, those rough-coated, savage creatures who guarded sheep and cattle and were said to be brave enough to tackle a wolf.

The news of this event was spread around well beforehand and since the Astallon acres were so far flung that some of them were two days' walk away, whole families began to arrive on the previous evening and were housed in the spaces where lately the knights' horses had waited. My Lord Astallon provided prodigious quantities of beef and bread and ale, for this was the season when all animals not needed for next year's breeding had to be slaughtered because there was not enough food to keep them alive through the winter.

It was now October but one of those still days that have something of summer lingering in them. The morning had been misty but it was clear and sunny when we took our places on the benches in the Ladies' Gallery. I looked around for Melusine and failed to find her. But presently one of my Lady's waiting women—the one called Catherine—edged along and spoke softly in Dame Margery's ear. Dame Margery said, 'If her Ladyship says so,' in no very pleased voice and then leaned over and said to Madge, 'You are invited to sit with the ladies.' She had to say it twice before Madge understood. Then she looked pleased and went along, falling over her feet and bumping into people, and took her seat with the grown-ups.

She was, after all, now fourteen and it was time she left us but seeing her go I wondered what would become of her in the grown-up world. It was unthinkable that she should become a lady-in-waiting to Lady Astallon or anyone else. She was very wealthy and had she been just a mite prettier somebody might have married her for her money; but she had no looks at all and was so plainly simpleminded that it would take a very hard man indeed to marry her. The reason would have been so clear. And though dozens of men did marry for money and dozens of girls were married for their money in this, as in everything else, people of the Beauclaire sort, as I called them, liked to put a good face on things.

I remember watching her blunder away and thinking what a good thing it would be if Dame Margery, instead of going to the Convent at Crowhurst, would retire with Madge to all those acres in Leicestershire and look after her and see that she was not cheated and did not forget to change her linen and things like that. Then, I thought, the Children's Dorter might break up and I could go back to Baildon and begin on my real life.

Then I forgot about everything because I was so sorry for the bear.

He was tethered and his nose had been cut to make him savage and so that the scent of blood might make the dogs savage.

I stopped being Maude Reed and became that bear. My nose hurt. And from my nose, pain ran all through me, settling low in my stomach as though I had been eating green apples.

It was a remarkably good bear. He threw off dog after dog. Every now and then I felt for the dogs, too. It was horrible.

The ordinary people were not allowed anywhere near us. Lady Astallon said she couldn't bear the stench of them, so they were gathered at both ends of the tourney ground and on the side opposite. On our side there were a number of gentlemen, all very excited, wagering with one another, mainly about how long a dog would last. 'I give him a count of five.' 'Seven!' 'Taken.' And so on. The gentlemen wagered in clinking coins; the ordinary people in goods— apples, eggs, chickens, even a young goat changed hands.

The scent of blood presently reached even the place where we sat and I saw my Lady Astallon dip her fingers into one of the bowls of that sweet-scented stuff and hold them, delicately, before her face and then pass it along.

Somebody shouted, 'Loose two dogs.' The bear dealt with them, gallantly and cleverly, though he was growing weary now. I felt his weariness in my bones.

Somebody cried, 'Only one dog left, my Lords and Ladies.'

I thought—Then it will soon be over and, despite all his wounds, the bear will have won.

Something dismal in my mind added, 'To do the same again, suffer the same, in another place on another day.'

That made me miserable enough. But then somebody shouted, 'Blind the bear. Bring pepper!'

After all that, to have pepper thrown in his eyes!

I had been at Beauclaire for a year, had been taught not to shout or yell or show temper.

But I yelled, louder than I had ever done in my life, and I moved more quickly. I roared, 'No! No!' and while I roared I saw the weapon I needed. The Tournament decorations had not been removed and into the rail at the foot of the Ladies' Gallery the pennants were still fixed, gaily-coloured little flags on pointed staves.

Dame Margery said, 'Maude. Maude Reed!' But I was already over the rail. Not for nothing had Henry Rancon and I practised jumping into and out of our saddles with our arms folded. I was over the rail and down on the tourney ground in one leap. My ankle stabbed. My silly head veil caught on a splinter of the rail but I threw it off, headdress and all. I snatched up the pennant and ran to join the bear who was part of me. Anybody who came to put pepper in his eyes would have me to deal with.

Dame Margery said later that I had lost my head. That was quite untrue. My head had never been better, for as I shouted against the pepper I also yelled, 'I will buy the bear. I will buy him. Who owns him?'

And standing there, feeling a loneliness even greater than I

had felt when I stepped into the Well Yard Room or the Long
Gallery on the day of my arrival, I was also grateful to my
grandfather, who had given me money, and to Henry Rancon,
who had made me active and quick.

The poor bear grovelled, thinking perhaps that he had failed
and would be beaten. He had been trained to fight dogs, to be
humble to human beings who had treated him so ill. From the
people I could feel not just the not caring which had troubled
me a year ago but something more, a definite hostility. I had
spoiled their game, ruined their bets.

To the shabby, furtive little man who came forward and said
the bear was his and named his price, I gave what he asked.
A high price but I had it. I unhooked the chain and said to the
bear, 'Come,' and he got up and shambled along. Where to put
him? What did bears eat? Outside the house the only place I
could be sure of was the bit of the stable where Brownie stood.
I took the bear there.

In the stable there was the same feeling of hostility. The
horses could smell the bear, the stranger, perhaps even the
blood. Brownie, who knew and, I thought, trusted me, snorted
and shuffled. It took me some time to quiet him. I chained
the bear up short, thinking that I knew nothing of his temper;
he might not be so meek when he recovered his strength. I
offered him oats and hay but they were not to his liking; so,
remembering that Brownie liked bread, I went to the kitchen
quarters to beg some. In fact, there was no need to beg, for all
the servants were on the tourney ground; so I helped myself
and took apples, too, to try. He ate both.

I had no wish to go back to the deserted house. I could hear,
from the tourney ground, the sound of laughter and applause
and guessed that the next entertainment had been hurried on. I
knew I was going to be in dire disgrace and I was beginning to
feel that I had made a fool of myself. I could just imagine what
Dame Margery would have to say. So I thought I would go
for a walk in the Maze. For us it was forbidden ground except
when in the company of a grown-up who knew the twists and
turns. Dame Margery had taken us into it once. It consisted of

dozens and dozens of little paths, all running into one another, all hedged with yew so high that when you were on one path you could not see into another. At the very centre there was a stone, carved all over with signs and marks. There were two stories told about the Maze. One was that an Astallon child, a boy, had wandered there and lost himself, had been overtaken by darkness and frozen to death. Perhaps that was true and accounted for the rule. The other was a kind of superstition. If you could make your way alone to the stone in the centre and wish and then find your way out again, unaided, your wish would come true.

I had a very desperate wish to make and I was in such a low state of mind that I felt that if I wandered there until I died it would not matter much.

I had taken perhaps half a dozen turns when, coming to a point where I must turn either left or right, I thought I heard voices. I had no wish to see anyone, so I peeped and there, just to my left, I saw my Uncle Godfrey and Melusine. They had their arms around one another and were kissing—not with butterfly kisses. I hastily backed up the path behind me and at its end took another turn, as it happened the right one, for presently I came to the place where four paths met and there in the centre was the stone.

They were far behind me now, so I spoke my wish aloud.

'I wish,' I said, 'I wish that something would happen to take me back to Baildon, soon.'

I do not think it was my imagination. It seemed to me that the sun went in and that it turned very cold, as though, instead of being a golden October afternoon, it was dusk on a winter day. I shivered and felt frightened and hastily made the sign of the Cross and said, 'God between me and all evil.' Then I turned and hurried back along the path by which I had come, hurrying to warm myself, hurrying to be out of the Maze, for I had decided after all that I did not wish to be benighted there, all alone in the dark. Better Dame Margery's scolding and any punishment she could inflict.

Then I did indeed lose my head. I forgot about the wish

working only if you got in and out again without help. I shouted for my uncle, for Melusine, for anybody. Nobody came. It grew darker and darker. The sky looked purple and the yew hedges black. My great dread was that any turn might bring me again to the centre and to the stone. But that did not happen. Suddenly I was at the entrance and could stop and get my breath and pull myself together. I could even think. I thought perhaps that wish was wasted; after this they may send me home.

'I have never, never in all my life,' Dame Margery said, 'seen any female make such a spectacle of herself. I have never been so much ashamed. A year of good training and you go galloping about like a wild pony and shouting like a fishwife.'

I said, 'I am sorry that I shamed you. Dame Margery.' I was sorry that she had taken it so much to heart. I waited to hear what punishment she had in store for me. When she did not name it, I thought, hopefully, 'That is because she has not the power to send me home in disgrace—that will be for my Lady Astallon to do.'

She scolded on and on. When I climbed the rail I had shown my legs to above the knee. I had made a vulgar display of wealth. When she said that, I felt bound to answer. 'Saying I would pay for the bear was all I could do. And how was that more vulgar than betting?'

'It was the way in which it was done.' She was inclined to say that kind of thing when she had no proper answer. Then she said, 'And you let poor Henry Rancon in for a beating.'

'I? Why should Henry be beaten? And what have I to do with it?'

'There were those who felt cheated,' Dame Margery said. 'They would have set about you and the man who sold the bear. But Henry Rancon took another pennant and threatened them.'

'That I did not know,' I said. But my heart warmed to Henry who had remembered that I was his liege and had come to my aid.

Perhaps more would have been made of this affair had not people's thoughts been directed to another matter.

It was the custom at Beauclaire for any announcement

concerning the household, or any bit of news that had drifted in from the outer world, to be made during supper. Very occasionally, if it concerned something like one of the Beauclaire knights winning a prize, for example. Lord Astallon would himself beat on the high table with his wine cup and speak.

More often, when it was some ordinary thing, the Steward would rise from his table, mount the platform and, standing behind his lord, speak, as it were, for him. Anything that had to do with the Chapel was, naturally, announced by the Chaplain, who would stand and remind us that such and such a day was a fast day and we must eat no meat or that since this or that of the outlying manors had had no priest for six months, he must go there to remind the people of their Christian duties and bury the dead, baptise a few babies or marry a few couples.

On the evening of the bear-baiting when the Chaplain stood up—unlike the Steward he did not have to climb onto the platform, he had his own place at the High Table—we all thought it was something of this kind which he had to say.

It was not. He stood up to say that Godfrey Blanchefleur, Knight, and Madge Fitz-Herbert, spinster, were betrothed in the sight of God.

A betrothal was not a marriage but it was almost as binding, and had the same solemnity.

'Go along,' Dame Margery said, and gave Madge a shove. From the Knight's table, my Uncle Godfrey stood up. The Chaplain came down from the High Table and stood in the little space between the platform and the end of the central table. There, obeying him, they joined hands.

I thought—Melusine! I looked toward the place where she sat with the other ladies.

What an example of self-control. She gave no sign at all. Like everyone else, she looked toward the couple thus suddenly betrothed. Like everyone else, she lifted her cup and drank, wishing them happiness.

Coming as it did at the end of a day of that sort—the bear; the Maze; the wish; the scolding—it was all too much for me.

I thought—Minsham Old Hall... those kisses in the Maze, only this very afternoon, now this! Something extremely strange happened inside my head, a spinning dizziness and then nothing; and then there was Dame Margery holding me, shaking me. 'Come along,' she said and, taking a firm hold on my arm, pulled me out of the hall and into the open air. I still felt very strange and I expected another scolding about lack of self-control. But she was very kind, helped me upstairs and into bed and brought me some cordial that was both fiery and sweet. When I felt better, I asked, 'What happened?'

'You swooned,' she said, 'and small wonder, after this afternoon's nonsense!'

'And now I have interrupted your supper,' I said penitently.

'I was not sorry to get away.' She twisted her hands together, always with her a sign of agitation. 'I never thought it would come to it, for all the talk,' she said in a voice of disgust. 'I thought they would surely see. I thought the man himself... Suppose,' Dame Margery said, no longer talking to me, 'she should have a child. Idiots breed idiots, as cows breed calves. Oh, I know that to a knight without land or money her wealth is a temptation but it should not have been allowed. They are all to blame; even the King. He should have given the poor child a pension, enough to keep her comfortable, and taken the land away. I am concerned for her. How can she stand up for herself? And once they are married I doubt if he will be kind.'

She was speaking to me of my own uncle but I shared her doubt. For one thing I could remember several occasions when my mother had been less than kind. To me, that is. She was always kind to Walter. And what could be said for a man who promised marriage and planned a future with one woman and had this in mind? Who could be giving Melusine hard kisses in the afternoon and at suppertime offer his hand to another? No, I thought, he will not be kind.

'Money,' Dame Margery said, still talking furiously to herself. 'That is all they think of. The whole system is rotten to the core. It will bring God's judgment on itself.'

When the war broke out and calamity came upon the great houses and the proud families and upon the King, I remembered my Dame's words but I lived long enough to see that in the end nothing was really changed.

I lay awake a long time that night, thinking of Melusine and her 'most secret secret,' which was nothing now. I thought of my own plans to have her as a neighbour, an aunt, a friend. All my plans were nothing now. I thought of my wish and wondered if it would be granted and, if so, in what form.

I also thought about the bear. Would he be allowed to remain in the stable? Would he, when he felt stronger, turn fierce? Would I be able to keep him alive on bread and apples? If he lived and remained friendly, how would I get him to Baildon when I went home?

When, at last, tired out, I fell asleep, I had a horrid dream. I dreamed that it was Walter who was lost in the Maze and very frightened. I knew the way, in and out, and was not frightened, so I kept calling to him, telling him to stay still and I would come and guide him. But he paid no attention and the calls grew farther and farther away, until I could not hear him at all.

However, I woke up bright and lively in the morning and at the first possible moment went out to the stable with the usual titbit for Brownie and food for the bear. There I was met by the boy who had taken my money in return for looking after my pony and I knew at once, by the way his lower lip stuck out, that he was displeased about something.

He said, 'I undertook to tend a pony, Mistress, not to go into a wild beast's cage.'

'That is reasonable,' I said. It was what my grandfather always said to one of his workmen who came with a genuine complaint. I went in. The stable, like everything else at Beauclaire, was arranged in order of importance; the great horses first, the quicker, lighter saddle horses, sometimes called nags, then the ponies and the hard-working donkeys who carried water and firewood.

Brownie greeted me in his usual manner, a little more eager than usual, for he had been neither fed nor watered. The bear lay exactly as I had left him, settled down to rest after eating the bread and the apple.

He was dead. Dead as stone. As dead as he might have been yesterday afternoon had I not interfered.

I was both sad and glad—sad that he would never know that he had changed hands and that whatever happened I meant to stand by him and treat him kindly; glad that I should not have to make any arrangements for him. At least he had not been blinded with pepper and thus blinded had to deal with that last dog. He had eaten the bread and the apple... I gave Brownie everything I had brought and said, 'Will can bring you water now.' And for a groat Will, I had no doubt, would drag the body away and put it on the midden, where all rubbish was thrown.

I said to the bear, 'Rest in Peace,' which was perhaps a wrong thing to say, since only souls can rest in peace and animals are supposed to have no souls. And then, suddenly, I realised that I was not alone. I whisked around quite ready to deny that I had said 'Rest in Peace' to a bear. I would say that whoever it was was mistaken and that I had said, 'Take this piece,' to Brownie. But it was not Will, the stable boy, or the Master of Stables come to order me and the bear out. It was Henry Rancon.

And what a transformation! I had not seen him on the previous afternoon, being in a state to notice nothing, but on the evening before I had seen him in the outgrown Astallon green. And Dame Margery had said that for taking sides with me he would be beaten. Now here he was, very gay in buff and tawny, all new and fitting well.

He said, and I knew that he felt as awkward as I did, reaching back into the old childish game, 'Sir Reed, I thought I might find you here. I came earlier and waited.'

I said, 'Sir Henry, I was given to understand that my behaviour yesterday afternoon had led you to misbehave too and gained you a beating.'

'No,' he said, 'it went the other way... Maude, my heart was with you, I could not bear... It was only a game but we were sworn and I could not bear to see you set upon. And there was a lord there, Lord Bowdegrave... he said I was wasted as a page, carrying dishes and messages; I should be a squire. So now I am.'

'So I see.'

'But for you I might have stayed a page for years and not been noticed, big and strong and eager as I am. You did me good service.'

'I am glad some good came of it. The bear is dead and I am in disgrace.'

Henry said, 'It was an old bear, due to die. And a bear would have been a trouble to you.' I knew he was trying to cheer me up and was grateful to him for that.

'When do you leave?' I asked.

'Today. Almost at once. I go with my new master to St. Albans.'

We stood, awkward again. Then I stuck out my hand and said,

'I hope that all goes well with you. Sir Henry.'

Instead of letting go my hand, he held it and slipped from his finger a ring, made of some base metal—lead, by the weight of it—with a little line of blue enamel running around it.

'Will you wear this, for memory?'

Such exchanging of tokens was common, so I said, 'Yes. I am sorry that I have nothing to give you.'

He said, and the words came out in a rush, 'Give me your word, Maude. Wait for me. Give me a chance. There is going to be a war and in war promotion comes earlier. I shall be Sir Henry in fact, and when I am I shall come to Baildon. It is Baildon?'

Something happened to me. I wanted to tell him that by that time I would be a wool merchant but all at once I could not speak. I thought—this is all part of the game. He'll go away and forget me in a fortnight and I shall forget him, except to remember that he was one of the few people I liked at Beauclaire. So I nodded. He pushed his head forward and kissed me. Most surprisingly, the lips in his weather-roughened face were as smooth and soft as silk.

CHAPTER VI

My lessons had been interrupted when the house emptied for the summer. Now they started again. Melusine had changed. She was just as kind as ever but less attentive. She would set me a copy and then sit, leaning her cheek on her hand and staring at the wall. When I had made my copy she would glance and say, 'That is well written,' but without really noticing or caring. Once I made a deliberate mistake; she did not remark that, either.

I waited for her to open the subject but she did not, so one day I said, 'It grieves me to the heart that one of my family—'

'Hush,' she said, 'we will not speak of that. It is over and must be forgotten.'

So the days went on, growing shorter and darker and colder, and one morning while I was at my lesson a servant came to say that someone was in the kitchen yard, asking for me. I jumped up. I thought—my wish has come true. Jack Plant has been sent to fetch me home.

The first snow of the year was falling that morning and as I sped through the kitchen I thought that they might have asked him in. I opened the door and there was my brother, Walter. I threw my arms around him and kissed him and brought him into the house, wondering all the time why he had been sent. My father had died young of the lung sickness and Mother always said Walter was delicate and must on no account catch cold.

He was less pleased to see me than I was to see him—or at least so it seemed—but with Walter you never knew.

I said, 'Have you come to fetch me?'*

'No. I have come to say good-bye.'*

'What do you mean?'

55

'I will tell you when we are alone.'

I took him along to the little room where I had lessons. There was a fire there and Melusine had gone.

I said, 'Tell me, Walter, what do you mean? We said good-bye when I left the Old Vine.'

'This is different. I have left the Old Vine too.'

Of course in fourteen months he had grown, as I had, but more and not sturdily. I saw that when he loosened the ties of the hooded coat he wore. Hood and coat were both made of sheepskin, the wool inside. With it tied about him he looked bulky; inside it, he still had that delicate look. We were twins but we were not at all alike—his hair and eyes were dark, my hair was reddish and my eyes were almost green. The gossip in the yard had said that my grandfather's second wife, our grandmother, had been a very strange kind of woman, a dancer, a woman of the roads upon whom he had taken pity, and it was true that Walter looked like nobody else I had ever seen.

I said, 'What do you mean, you have left the Old Vine?'

'I had to. Maude, we have only one life and I could not spend mine there. I told them and told them but they would not listen. Every night in the same bed, every day at the same table and on and on until life ends, with all the world to see. I could bear it no longer. I came away.'

'When?'

'It was high summer. I went first to Walsingham, with the pilgrims, then to Lynn and Lincoln. I earn my way, Maude. I play my lute and I sing. I am now on my way to Canterbury and being so near...' He waved one of his delicate hands and I saw that the other clutched his lute, wrapped in cloth, to his side, inside the loosened coat.

I said, 'But Walter, this is crazy talk. To put yourself on the open road as a strolling player. And winter setting in...'

Suddenly I saw what I thought was the truth. In his curious way he had relied on me; he had run from home and now was sorry and had come to me, trusting me to make peace.

And that I could not very well do without going back to Baildon. So my wish had been granted.

I said, 'It will be all right, Walter. We will go back together and I will explain. I still have some money. I'll buy you a pony...'

Walter said, 'Just like the rest of them—I'll buy this, I'll buy that; settle down, go home, be good; put that lute away and count fleeces... I thought better of you, Maude. I looked to you for a glimmer of understanding. Grandfather reasoned with me and offered me bribes for four hours. Mother wept for six. Then he said, 'Go. Come back when you are hungry.' And she said, 'Go. You have broken my heart.' And I was sorry. But when the road calls... Maude, to have nothing, nothing but the lute one can play and the song one can sing... such freedom ... It is difficult to imagine, I know, but I thought you might understand.'

I said, 'And they let you go?' Grandfather's reasoning and Mother's weeping I could well understand, but not their letting him go.

'What choice had they?' Walter asked, and he threw up his head and took on a look I had noticed before, as though he were facing a wind blowing against him. 'They could have locked me up, I suppose, and made Master Firman my keeper instead of my tutor, but what good would that have done? In any case, he wanted me away. Between you and me, he has his eye on the business. And that is—besides my wish to take leave and to be understood—my reason for coming here, Maude. I do not want, I do not mean to have anything to do with sheep or wool or weaving or with land. But suppose the old man, our grandfather, should die. I am his legal heir. Lying out under hedgerows and haystacks all this summer, I have considered this thing... I shall not be there, for when I have seen England and perhaps looked into Wales, I intend to go to Provence where all the best tunes and the best songs are made. I would like it to be set down in writing and properly witnessed that anything due to me in the way of inheritance should be yours.'

I said, 'Walter, do not speak of such a thing. I know, I have always known, that you had no fondness for the business but I would run it for you. I always thought of you sitting indoors and warm while I saw to things. I was born a wool merchant; you were born a lute player. We could share.'

'And live in Baildon?'

'But of course.'

'You understand as little as the others. I have gypsy blood in me, Maude. To stay in one place, see the same faces, hear the same talk, eat the same food...'

That word reminded me, and I said, 'Are you hungry now, Walter?'

He said, 'I am always hungry nowadays. And that is as it should be.' At home he had never had much appetite.

In a place like Beauclaire it was impossible to get a proper meal at a makeshift hour but I fetched him a piece of bread and honey and some apples and told him that dinner would soon be served and that I would ask Dame Margery if he could sit at our table. 'There is to be suckling pig,' I said. I had seen and smelled it cooking.

'I don't want it,' Walter said, 'at the price of being known. Mistress Reed's mad brother who has run from home and taken to the road. Naughty boy who should be chided and sent home.'

'But that is what you are.'

'I did not come here to argue, Maude. I know what I am. Who in this place can write his name?' He said 'this place' with a kind of scorn, not impressed by its size or its splendour.

'The Lady Melusine,' I said. 'She taught me. And the Chaplain, I suppose.'

'Then we will get this signed and I will be on my way. Unless they need a musician at dinner. In that case I will eat suckling pig and give value for it.'

He had, of course, no idea of how things were done in great houses. I could have asked Dame Margery for permission to bring my brother to our table but who was I to order the Chaplain, or Melusine, or to arrange for music in the dining hall? But there was Walter, trusting me, as always, to deal with the practical side of things.

He took from inside the cloth that wrapped his lute a piece of parchment, rather smaller than the one on which he had written his Christmas Piece. There was writing on it, very small and even; the border and the capital letters were not decorated. I had just time to read, 'This deed witnesseth that I, Walter Reed…' Then Walter said, 'Well, run along. Fetch them. They are supposed to see me sign.'*

So I had no choice.

Melusine came willingly enough; the Chaplain, though I apologised most humbly for disturbing him, was first grumpy and then curious. 'What document? What is this all about?' he asked as we went through cold passages and up and down draughty stairways. I remembered that Walter had said about not wishing to be known as Mistress Reed's brother, so I simply said, 'It is a document to be signed and witnessed, sir.'

In the little room Walter did nothing to ease curiosity or soothe irritation. When the Chaplain said, 'What is this?' Walter said, 'Something I have put in writing and wish to put my hand to before witnesses. There is no need to read it.'

'I could not, it is written so small. Who wrote this?'

'I did.'

'What is it?'

'A deed of gift. It concerns some property.'

'Yours?'

'Not yet. What will be mine one day.'

'This is highly irregular. No one can will away what he does not yet own.'

'I know that,' Walter said with insolent weariness. 'This is not a will. All I am asking is that you should witness that what is written was done by my hand. As it is. Here, I take the pen.' He took up the quill with which I had been copying, tried it on his thumb, and dipped it into the ink. 'And here I write my name.' He did so, this time the letters big and bold. The Chaplain seemed aghast at such behaviour from a mere boy, a stranger, but he wrote his name—Richard Frankland, Priest. And then, as he was about to hand the pen to Melusine, he said, 'I am not sure about the validity of a lady's signature in such a case. So few ladies can write.'

'Then I will not write my whole name,' Melusine said. She

wrote 'M. Talbot,' and said, 'They can take that for Mark or Matthew, as they will.'

'I thank you both,' Walter said, pleasant, satisfied, well disposed toward them now, almost lordly. 'In return I am prepared, if invited, to make merry music while you dine.'

I looked helplessly from one to the other. Melusine said nothing, for what went on in the way of entertainment in the dining hall she had as little power or responsibility as I had. But the Chaplain said, 'That would be good. My Lady Astallon was complaining only yesterday that as the roads and the weather worsened, players and mummers seemed to hibernate, like squirrels. Come with me...'

Walter took up his lute in his left hand, the parchment in his right. Following the Chaplain out, he put his right hand behind him and half turned his head.

'Take care of it,' he said. 'It may yet serve you.' And then he was gone, casting me off as he had cast off our grandfather, our mother, the house at Old Vine, the sheepruns and the pack ponies and the weaving sheds.

I was left for a moment with Melusine who, in the ordinary way, would have asked about him, who he was, where he came from, why did his signature matter, why had he handed the parchment to me. But she showed no interest and no curiosity. I should have known then. But I did not. I simply thought that the Chaplain would arrange for Walter to play and Walter would eat well before moving on to Canterbury.

And, of course, when Walter said, 'I know what I am,' he had spoken the truth. What he was was the best lute player and maker of songs then alive on earth and in a way, that day at Beauclaire, he had recognition, applause, calls for more. He was asked up onto the platform on which the High Table stood and my Lady Astallon gave him a sweetmeat with her own hands. And he scorned them all. Perhaps I was the only one who could see that but it was there. As he had scorned Baildon, the family and the business, so he scorned this great house and the people in it—to have the lute to play, the song to sing... for him that was enough. His way was his way. With

his lute in his hand and his song on his lips, he was free as a
bird or a flower.

When he had gone, speeded on his way with a warm
recommendation to the Archbishop of Canterbury, I settled
down to think things over. Walter had said that he had left
Baildon in high summer, at least three months ago. So there
was my grandfather, his grandson gone; my mother with no
child. But they had not sent for me. There, I thought, sat my
grandfather, thinking that Walter's was only a summer folly
—'Go. Come back when you are hungry'—a practical man
who in his time had known hunger. And my mother, saying—
'Go, you have broken my heart,'—thinking that the child
she cared for, her beloved son, would remember, would pity,
would return when his itch for the open road was satisfied by
a pilgrimage to Walsingham which, after Canterbury, was the
most sacred place in England.

I imagined them there, lonely and waiting... waiting for the
boy who would not come back. Would my grandfather think—
There is Maude? Would my mother think—I have lost my
son but I have a daughter? It seemed not. No word came from
Baildon and I thought, they do not want me, and was sad.

This year, as the days closed in, there was not only Christmas
to think of—there was the wedding. In the ordinary way, had
poor Madge had parents, she would have been home by now
and her mother would have overlooked the preparation, the
wedding gown, the wedding feast. As it was, all was to be done
at Beauclaire and worked in with the Christmas festivities.

Dame Margery seemed to have resigned herself and took us
out into the woods to collect the holly, the mistletoe and the ivy
with which the garlands and decorations must be made. The
Yule Log, which must be stout and thick enough to burn all
through the Twelve Days of Christmas, had already been cut
and was being hauled over the drawbridge as we went out to
bring in as much greenery as we could carry.

It was a sullen day, the sky and the moat the colour of
unpolished pewter and a shrewd little wind blowing from the
east. The woods were dumb. Servants had gone ahead of us,

doing all the real work— the climbing and the hacking—and all we had to do was to fill our arms, bring in our token offerings in order to please Dame Margery's sense of what should be done, year after year. The rest could be left to men.

So we filled our arms and when Dame Margery said, 'Sing, it will warm you,' we sang 'The Holly and the Ivy,' and 'Jesus, sweet dear son, on a poor bed thou liest,' and other carols.

And there we were, our arms full of what was to make Christmas cheerful and carols on our tongues as we came back over the drawbridge. And to the left of us a group of men stood, busy and bustling. William Rancon said, 'They have dropped the Yule Log. Look, they have rope and grapple.'

So they had but what, as we halted and watched, they brought up was not the Yule Log. It was Melusine.

The hooks of the grapple had taken her by the middle and she came out of the cold, dull water in a curve, her feet hanging, and her long, silver-gilt hair...

'Come, come, come,' Dame Margery said, bustling around us like a sheep dog.

I began to cry, I who had not shed a tear in the year and a quarter I had been at Beauclaire. And once having started, I could not stop. At first Dame Margery was kind and said, 'Oh yes, of course, she taught you. Well, cry a little and ease your grief.' Then she lost patience and said, 'This is no way to make ready for Christmas.' That made me cry more, thinking of all the Christmases Melusine would never see. So pretty, so gay and so kind.

And why did she do it? I could see that all her secret hopes and plans had been ruined; but she had borne up bravely then and rather more than two months had passed. One outlives disappointment. Was it, I wondered, that she could not bear to see my uncle and Madge married? I went on crying and at last Dame Margery said, 'Now look here; enough is enough. That will do. I will not have you cry yourself sick over that wicked woman.' That did stop me. I said, 'What do you mean? Wicked? Melusine never did a wicked thing in her life. She was the kindest, sweetest...' Dame Margery made a face as though she had eaten a sour plum. 'She took her own life, did she not? That is a deadly sin. Life is from God and only He may end it.'

I said, 'God will forgive her. He knows she had reason.'

At that, Dame Margery gave me a very peculiar look indeed.

Everybody seemed to be of Dame Margery's opinion. To commit suicide was a mortal sin. They did not even give her a proper funeral or a grave in hallowed ground. I did not even know when, or how, or where she was buried. Melusine was shuffled away so that the Christmas merriment to which, this year, was added the extra gaiety of the wedding, could begin.

I woke in the dark of Christmas morning and knew that I could not face it—the dancing, the feasting, going on for twelve days; and on the third day Constance, Helen, Alison and I having to act as ladies-in-waiting to the bride, poor Madge.

I lay there and made my plan—the only kind of plan that ever comes to anything, the kind that depends upon you alone. That, at least, was something I had learned—any plan that concerns another person may easily go wrong.

And wishing was no good either. I had solemnly wished that something might happen to get me home to Baildon and nothing had. I was too stupid then to see the truth.

CHAPTER VII

For anyone wanting to do something out of the ordinary, Christmas was the best time to choose because for the twelve days everything was in an uproar and nobody had a mind for anything but pleasure. Brownie and I trotted over the drawbridge without attracting any attention. I gave one look at the place from which Melusine had been hauled out of the moat and the tears started again. Then I told myself that I had a long way to go, very likely some danger to face and that crying would do no good. My grandfather had told me that and I had not heeded. But between hearing and heeding a thing and knowing it, inside yourself, there is a difference. Now I knew.

I had travelled this road at the end of a long, hot summer when the road was a track of dust. Now it was muddy. The snow that had begun to fall on the day of Walter's visit had stayed for a while, then melted. Since then there had been some frost and after that, rain. Brownie and I held to the crown of the road, the best part, but even that was not good. However, he was surefooted and I did not hurry him. In the Beauclaire stable, doing for myself, putting on the saddle and the bridle, I had said, 'Brownie, we are going home.' He may not have understood me—how much do they know? After all, you can take a pigeon with such a little head, so much smaller than a pony's, to France and let it loose and it will make for home. And there was something about the way Brownie went, plodding in the mud, trotting where the road had been made up at some time by somebody throwing a few barrowloads of stone onto it, that gave me the idea that he did know.

I had dressed myself warmly and brought with me all I had of value—the rest of my grandfather's money gift, my pearl-

and-gold pin, a few other simple ornaments. I had brought
Walter's document and his Christmas Piece and the last copy
that Melusine had ever set me. For myself I had a loaf of raisin
bread, for Brownie a bag of oats.

I was desperately afraid of robbers, the more so because at
this season I was unlikely to find company on the road. All
good, honest people with a roof over their heads and a fire to
sit by would be at home, keeping Christmas as best they could.
I also knew that when I neared home and reached the part of
Essex and Suffolk where the woods stood thick, I would be
afraid of wolves. They were less numerous than they were
because there had been some effort made to do away with them
by offering a reward to anyone who could produce a wolf's
head and tail; but they were still plentiful enough and in winter
they grew bold through hunger. However, it was of no use to
think about danger or worry beforehand.

When I judged by the light that it was about midday, I began
looking around for water, a stream or a pool, and when I found
a stream I drank from my cupped hands, let Brownie drink,
gave him a handful of oats and cut myself a slice of the loaf. I
walked about a bit to stretch my legs and let him rest. Then I
remounted and rode on. The day began to darken and in a day's
journey I had seen perhaps a dozen people, all in villages, all
afoot, all going, it was plain, to visit a near neighbour on this
Christmas Day.

I began to look for an inn in which to spend the night. And there,
as with the stream, I was lucky. Inns were easily recognised, for
they hung out signs, very often a simplified version of the coat-
of-arms of the lord to whom the innkeeper paid his rent. When
you saw some great man's badge outside a humble building, that
was the inn and often enough there was also a bush, uprooted and
hung over the door. I came to a crossroads which I remembered
from my journey with the horrid Astallon man.

There was a gibbet at one corner. It had been empty when
we passed it on my way to Beauclaire. Now it was occupied,
a body hanging from its single arm and swaying in the wind.
A murderer perhaps, or a thief, but to be honest, I did not

think much about him. What I did think was that, since at this crossroads men were hanged, though the place seemed lonely and deserted now, there would be times when there were crowds and where there were crowds, there was likely to be an inn somewhere nearby. And I was right. Only a short distance along one of the side roads there was a little house with a badge, a white hart, over the door and what had once been a green bush but now looked like a bunch of firewood.

It was kept by a man who had lost a leg in the French wars and by his wife. They seemed to be amazed—but pleased—to have a guest on Christmas Day. They were plainly very poor. 'Nobody comes in winter,' the woman told me. 'Nobody's been since Bob Shotley was strung up. Six, seven weeks ago. A great day that was. We killed two geese and broached a barrel of ale.' Her husband had hobbled away to stable Brownie and she seemed glad to have somebody to talk to. 'And all the time the taxes go up,' she said, 'whether you do much trade or not.' I let her talk. I made sympathetic noises and perhaps there I made my mistake, for presently she said, 'You're full young to be out on your own, Mistress.'

I said, 'I am much older than I look. I was on a visit and was called home. My grandfather is ill and it being Christmas it was not convenient for anyone to ride with me.' I thought that I didn't want any more questions or remarks about the oddity of my being out alone, so I said, 'What are you going to give me for supper?'

'What we had for dinner, only it was hot then.' Their Christmas dinner had been belly pork, striped fat and lean, more fat than lean. When she brought it out, I said, 'I want very little. One thin slice will do.' The bread which she had also brought out was very dark and coarse.

Her husband came back and told me how he had lost his leg and what a handicap it was to be obliged to hobble about on a wooden peg. He also told me that trade was bad and taxes went up all the time. Then he said one thing which did please me, simple fool that I was, 'That's a nice little pony. Mistress. Strong as a lion, gentle as a lamb.'

The bed they gave me was horrible, but I slept well on it. I was on my way home... I actually fell asleep thinking of what I should say and what would be said to me when at last Brownie trotted into the yard at Old Vine and he made for his stable and I must face my grandfather, who would understand a bit, and my mother, who would scold. At least... unless Walter's going had broken her down and she would be glad to see her one remaining child. That, to be honest, was what I counted on.

I rose in the morning and broke my fast on a bit of the almost black bread and a mug of goat's milk. I had paid overnight and had only to say good-bye to the woman and go out to the wretched little stable where the man had saddled Brownie. He was very civil. He asked me which way I was riding and I told him. I said, 'I know I have to go back to the crossroads and make for the north. I remember the road.' I was civil, too. Although I had paid for it, I thanked him for his hospitality and he in turn wished me Godspeed.

So, on the second day of Christmas, there we were, Brownie and I, trotting along, heading for home at a pace which, though it might seem slow to the Astallon man on his tall horse, actually ate up the miles. Again at midday I looked for and found water. We both drank, he ate oats, I ate raisin bread. And on this day my misery, the feeling—'I can have no more of this!' began to ease. My grief for Melusine and my hatred for those who thought her wicked faded a little. Not entirely, never entirely, but being out, being free, even being a little frightened and a little concerned as to how and where I should spend this night, acted on my soul's hurt in the same way that a bag of hot bran acted on earache. I felt better. I was beginning to look about me again for some place in which to spend the night when behind me I heard hoofbeats. I turned in my saddle and saw, bearing down on me, coming rapidly, a very curious shape: a horse with two humps. Of course, I thought, a man and a woman riding pillion. Lucky again, I thought; now maybe I shall have company on the road.

The horse overtook me and fell in alongside, blowing—a horse somewhat overpressed, glad to slow down. And its burden was not a man with a woman riding pillion, it was an old man with a big basket. He said, 'Good day, Mistress. Do we ride the same way?'

'Good day—good evening, rather. How can I tell? In which direction do you ride?'

'To Walsingham,' he said. 'That may sound strange, it not being the season for pilgrimage to that shrine. But I give a service to those who are too old or too infirm to make the journey. So in winter, when the roads are clear, I make the journey and carry back to them the holy water.'

I thought to myself, lucky indeed. A mounted man whose road took him within a few miles of Baildon, an old man, a greybeard, dealing with holy things.

I said, 'I am for Baildon. The Walsingham road skirts it by about four miles. If we could ride thus far together, it might be a convenience to us both.'

'And safer, too. For you. Mistress. You see, I wear this.'

He pointed to the cockleshell on his hat, sure sign that he was one of those who had made the journey to the Holy Land. 'It would take a very hardy rogue to raise hand against me.'

I thought—Not only protection but good company. As we travel he can tell me about his journeys.

'I was beginning to look for a place to sleep,' I said. I thought that if he used this road regularly he should know of a good clean inn.

'You mean an inn?' he asked. 'Alas, little Mistress, if you are one to use inns, we cannot travel together. I am a poor man. I sleep under the stars.'

'In this cold weather? It would be better... I mean, if you would not be offended by the suggestion... so long as we travel together and so long as my money lasts... if you would allow me to pay for your lodging.'

He thought this over. Then he said, 'I am not offended but it would be a sorry waste of money. I have learned how to make myself comfortable, even in the coldest night. I could make you comfortable too. And then, if you liked,' he spoke diffidently, 'I would take the money you had saved and offer it to Our Lady of Walsingham in your name. You would thus acquire virtue.'

I thought that over. 'I think I would sooner sleep under a roof. Later on I will remember and send Our Lady of Walsingham a gift.'

'Try my way, once,' he said coaxingly, 'and I'll warrant you will never wish to sleep in an inn again. But please yourself, of course. Inns do not suit me. Bad food and horrible beds. And when I wake I like to be on my way. Sometimes the stable is locked and one must wait for the landlord to wake and unlock it. Find a place to your taste. I shall sleep out and start off in the morning as suits me.'

That left me with no choice if I wished for his company, as I did, since I was unlikely to fall in with so suitable a fellow traveller again. I did say, 'What about supper? I have only a piece of plum loaf left.'

'I am well provided. I have ham and bread and cheese. I even have wine. People are charitable toward those who wear this and are in a position to pray for them at the holiest place in England, not excepting Canterbury.'

'Very well,' I said. 'I will try it your way.'

'Then we look, not for an inn but a straw stack.' We found one, just in time, for the light was going.

'We camp on the lee side,' he said. For all his grey hair and beard, he was nimble and moved quickly about, making a little fire for light and warmth, digging into the bottom of his basket and producing his provisions.

I said, 'I am a little worried about my pony. He has never spent a night except in a stable; he might stray.'

'Fasten him to my horse. She will stand till Judgement Day if left alone.' I gave both horses some of the oats. Then I sat down to what, after my meal the previous evening, seemed like a feast.

I said, 'Should we not leave some for tomorrow?'

'I have lived long enough to let tomorrow take care of itself. I am not ashamed to beg when I go on such an errand and it is still the Christmas season, when those who have food will share

it. If all else fails tomorrow, we can make do with your loaf.'
That reminded me that tonight I was eating his food, drinking
his wine. I said, 'Tomorrow I will buy food for us both. Tell me
something about your pilgrimage to the Holy Land.'

'Now that,' he said, 'we will leave for tomorrow. It is time
for sleep now.'

He made two little nests in the side of the straw stack, by
pulling out some trusses. 'Wrap your cloak around you well,'
he said. 'Creep in and pull the loose straw over your feet. I
hope you will sleep well.'

I thought I should, for a most unusual drowsiness had crept
over me, and in fact the nest in the straw was more comfortable
than the bed I had occupied on the previous night. I fell asleep
almost at once and did not wake until dawn.

I woke to disaster. The man and both horses had gone. So
had the pouch in which I carried my money and my trinkets. It
must have taken skill to remove that, for I had prudently tied
it around my waist inside my skirt. But it was gone; and there
I was, with nothing in the world left to me except the clothes I
wore and three pieces of parchment.

Then I remembered how much the one-legged man had
admired Brownie. I saw it all. I had not actually shown my
pouch at the White Hart but I had paid their charge without
quibble. A girl, travelling alone, with some money and a good,
strong, well-trained pony. An open invitation to villainy.

I went out into the road and studied the hoof-marks in the
mud. Just at the edge of the field in which the straw stack stood
they were muddled but on the road itself it was easy to see
that my Walsingham pilgrim had not gone north; there were
no hoof marks in that direction. He had turned back on his
tracks, thinking, no doubt, how easily he had fooled me and
counting upon his share of what had been in my pouch and
what Brownie would fetch.

I thought, you don't know me; I'll have my pony back if it's
the last thing I do. If necessary, I will go back to Beauclaire
and humble myself completely—that inn is only a day's ride
distant, my Lord Astallon will know the lord to whom the

badge of the White Hart belongs…

I hitched up my skirt and set out on the long trudge back to the crossroads where the gibbet stood.

CHAPTER VIII

Fortunately for me, our game of playing at being knights and squires had not been all jousting or all fun. Henry Rancon was so serious in his aims and his ambitions that he had set himself endurance tests, in which I had felt compelled to compete. Explained to any grown-up they would have seemed ridiculous but Henry would say, 'Now suppose we were on Crusade in a land without water. How long could we last? I think I could go three days.' Then I would say I thought I could, too. In that contest I did a little better than he did. We neither of us managed three days—he drank, looking terribly ashamed, at dinner on the second day and I held out until suppertime.

In addition to such tests, there were practices of skill, including one called 'Spying out the Land.' A fighting knight, which was what Henry intended to be, must be prepared to take advantage of natural things—horses, for example, charged better going downhill than uphill; surprise was a valuable weapon, so a good knight looked for cover.

They were childish games but in a way they served me now when I was obliged to cover, on foot, the journey that I had covered yesterday on a steady-trotting pony. First I spied out the land. In this area the land was all cultivated, the great fields divided into strips, one peasant's strip divided from another by a narrow bit of unploughed land, called a balk. I plodded along until I saw to one side of the road a little hillock, about twice the height of a house. The cultivated land stopped short at the foot of it and it was covered with blackberry and wild rose brambles.

I thought, this is a test of endurance, and forced my way to the top of it. In places I had to use my knife to hack myself a way and it was hard going, but well worth it. From the top I could look down and see the road I had travelled yesterday snaking and curving, and I could see the ploughed land and the pasture and the ground lying fallow, and I saw that if I did not keep to the looping road, if I struck straight, walking on the narrow but solid balks, I could perhaps cut my journey by a third. And if I ran, I might on foot do the pony's day journey in one day.

But it was hard going and I was obliged to cheer myself, toward the end, by taking refuge in fantasy. I was not Maude Reed, robbed and cheated; I was Sir Reed, a noble knight going to the rescue of some demoiselle in distress. That was Brownie, who would certainly be in distress by now. I had been unhorsed and disarmed; I had nothing but myself and my determination. But they both held.

My false companion had even taken what remained of my plum bread, so all that day I ate nothing but a little after midday I found the stream which I thought—not being quite sure— Brownie and I drank from yesterday. I drank from it again and hurried on.

By sunset I was at the crossroads where Bob Shotley, whoever he was, swung on the gibbet and, a little too near him for comfort, I sank down, completely exhausted, and pulled my thoughts together.

All through the day I had been borne up, I now realised, upon two props, neither of them real or sure. There was the suspicion of the one-legged innkeeper and my game about being Sir Reed. They had brought me so far but what now? Right down to bedrock, I saw that I had as yet no proof of what I suspected. The false pilgrim might have nothing to do with the couple at the White Hart and I most certainly had nothing to do with a mythical knight. Sir Reed, who had played in the Low Garden and the woods about Beauclaire with another mythical knight.

I was a stupid girl, robbed of everything. A foolish, headstrong creature who had come to grief and well deserved to do so.

That was the worst moment of all… and sitting there on the

little bank by the wayside, I realised how Melusine had felt and what had made her do what she did.

I was luckier, because in the middle of it all, I did care about Brownie. So I fought off self-doubt and despair and I kept my eye on the White Hart.

There was the faintest light. I knew it came from a dip no thicker than my little finger, a reed dipped into tallow, not a candle. I sat there, freezing and hungry, and presently I watched it move, the faint light from behind the unglazed window at ground level moving up the few stairs, lighting for a moment or two the higher window, and then it was quenched.

I waited. I said ten Paternosters and ten Hail Marys. I wanted to give them time to get sound asleep, so I curbed my impatience, though every minute seemed an hour. But at last I crossed the lane and walking as though I were blind, feeling with my hands, found the end of the wretched little house and so the way into the yard and to the stable. It was not locked. Before I had the door open I could hear Brownie, greeting me, blowing through his nostrils and making little soft whinnying noises. He was trying to tell me that he had had a horrible day, too.

On the evening before, by the straw stack, I had unsaddled him. The man who had stolen him and the one-legged man had not even bothered to do that — bad horsemanship indeed.

I led him out of the horrible place and trusting his eyes rather than my own, got back to the crossroads and did not take the way to Baildon for fear of being followed again. I took the side road and we stumbled along in the thick darkness, both dead tired and both hungry. Every now and then Brownie nudged me, asking for his tidbit. 'I have nothing for you,' I explained, 'but I will get you something tomorrow.' How? How?

Oddly enough, the idea of going back to Beauclaire did not occur to me then. I would have done it, I would have eaten humble pie in order to get Brownie back but for no other reason. So there I was, in the dark and the cold, without money or food and on the wrong road!

That was the longest and most uncomfortable night I have

even spent. The road ran downward presently and there the
wind seemed less. I thought this was as sheltered a spot as we
were likely to find. So I halted there. I tried to rest by leaning
against Brownie, who was at least warm. I put my arms round
his neck and leaned against his shoulder. But human beings
cannot sleep on their feet. I was so tired that despite the cold
I kept dozing off and then my hold on him relaxed and I'd
slip down. Then I'd lie where I'd fallen for a little while, glad
to be prone, until I thought of all the stories I had heard of
people who fell asleep and froze to death; such memories made
me get up and hug Brownie again; and so it went on. Once I
thought—if ever I see Henry Rancon again I will tell him about
an endurance test he never thought of!

But, like everything else, that night did at last come to an
end. With the first peep of light I mounted and we jogged along.
I tried to keep a look out for anything that would be useful—a
house at which I could beg, a haystack from which I could steal
a few handfuls for Brownie or a road that turned off to the left,
for I had taken the road that led eastward and must, sooner or
later, get back on to the one that went to Baildon.

Brownie, I guessed, had had nothing since that last handful
of oats I had given him. He began to flag, too. If it had been
ordinary countryside there might just have been a nibble of
grass but it was not. On either side of us, as far as I could see,
there was nothing but dead bracken and gorse bushes. The only
comforting thing was that although I came upon no definite
turn in the road, the road itself veered to the left and I guessed
that it now ran about parallel with the one I should have been
on. And once or twice we came upon a hole in the road with
enough water in it for Brownie to drink.

By midday, what with lack of food, lack of sleep and with
worry, I was getting a bit light-headed. I thought—somebody
should sing a song or tell a tale about a knight who set out
to rescue a demoiselle in distress and did it and then starved
to death, the rescued maiden with him. The road took another
curve to the left and ahead of me there were some trees, not
large, hawthorns, all grown sideways, bent by the wind that

blew from the east; and I thought I could smell cooking. Who would be cooking in this desolate land? I reckoned that I had nodded off to sleep in the saddle and dreamed the smell. But it was true.

There was a sound of voices and of laughter and just past the next clump of hawthorns I came upon them: six women... a good fire between three stout poles planted so that they met in the middle. And hanging from the point where the three poles joined, a goose, roasting. A little way away, three other geese were tethered to a bush.

There was no need to check Brownie. He slowed of his own accord, sensing that the sound and smell of people meant food, meant getting back to ordinary life.

I had never begged in my life, having had no need to. Now I must. I dismounted and, holding Brownie's rein, said, 'Good people, of your charity... a mouthful for me and if you have a crust of bread for my pony...'

Their behaviour showed something about the state of the country. They scented danger instantly, jumped up and grabbed at sticks thick enough to be cudgels. Their faces set into hard expressions of distrust and suspicion and fear. I admit my appearance was against me; I was caked with mud and what hair showed from inside my hood had not been combed for four days.

One of them—I knew later that she was called Emma, said, 'Who is with you?'

'Nobody. I am alone.' About the loneliest person in the world, I thought.

Emma said, 'Take a look.' Four women stepped onto the road. Two went in one direction; two in another.

Waiting, Emma said, 'Who are you? How do you come to be here?'

I told her my name and the story about being called home suddenly, travelling alone because of the season. 'And I was robbed of all I had.'

The woman with Emma said, 'That's a likely tale!'

'Nevertheless, true.'

'And where's this place you're making for?'

I had no reason to trust them entirely. I said, 'Suffolk.'

'Name of Reed?' Emma said. 'Who's your kin there?'

'My grandfather's name is Martin Reed.'

'And what's his trade?'

'He is a wool merchant,' I said.

She nodded. 'That's right. So he is. And an honest man.'

'You know him?'

'I know of him. All right, you're welcome to a bite of dinner.'

The other women came back and said that so far as they could see the road was empty.

Emma said, 'She's all right, I reckon,' and laid down her cudgel and took a knife and prodded the cooking goose. 'Ready, I'd say.' She took one of the poles, two other women took one each and they lifted the whole contraption off the fire. From one of the many baskets which stood around, one woman took a loaf and cut thick slices. It was good bread, too, almost white. Emma cut into the still sizzling goose flesh and laid a chunk on each slice.

I said, 'I am grateful to you and if you will tell me your names and where you live, my grandfather will see that you are repaid. Could you spare a bit of bread for my pony?'

'I don't hold with giving folks' food to horses,' one of the women said. 'He can have some of the meal.' They had a little sackful. She put some into a bowl, mixed it with water and stirred it with her hand. The geese, thinking it was for them, screamed with excitement and then, seeing it given to Brownie, with disappointment.

I thanked God that we had both been fed this day. We were indeed fortunate to have fallen in with them. They were goose-women, on their way back from London, where they had driven up a great flock of geese for the Christmas market. They had been on the road for weeks, travelling at the geese's pace, carrying food for themselves and their flock, sleeping on the bare ground and regarding it all as a holiday. They were a band and always travelled together. They came from different villages, all from the south of Suffolk, and were known as the

77

Bures Band because Emma lived in that village and it was there that they assembled their flocks. Each woman might be driving geese belonging to perhaps a dozen families. Not one of them could read or write but they could reckon perfectly. In London trade was done with money, not barter, and they all knew exactly what was owing to their neighbours. They travelled on this road because they regarded it as safer. 'Not that we can't give a good account of ourselves, if needs be,' they said. When I told them about the man with the cockleshell in his hat, who robbed me, they roared with laughter. Fancy being so simple as to be taken in by that!

Once we had eaten, they packed up briskly. The three remaining geese—their walking larder—went into a basket with a lid. As one of the women was preparing to hitch it onto her back, I said, 'My pony could carry that.' But it was difficult to fix it to the saddle, so we gave Brownie two baskets, roped together and slung across, like panniers, one on each side. I walked with the women and took my turn in carrying the rest of the loads.

I could not have happened upon better company. They knew the road from Bures to London and back as they knew their own backyards—they had their regular stopping places and they knew every trick for making a harsh way of life as comfortable as possible. We slept that night in an old chalk pit. They carried four rugs between them. Two were spread on the ground, two were used as covers and they slept there together, a good way of keeping warm. 'There's room for a little 'un,' Emma said, 'shove over, Amy.' And she made a space for me.

Sometimes as we trudged we sang, the favourite song being rather unseasonal—'Summer is a-coming in.' They exchanged simple jokes and stories that made them laugh but of which I often missed the point. They talked about people unknown to me, sometimes maliciously, and on that journey at least one marriage was arranged. Emma described her son—the prospective bridegroom—as a good boy but awkward. 'Not having a father he didn't get enough stick, though I did my best. Now he's taken it into his head that he must see a girl before he'll say he'll marry her.'

'My Mary'll stand a bit of looking over,' Amy said with motherly pride. 'She's been offered for but he wasn't a Suffolk man and I didn't want her to live too far away. If she married your Robin, I'd see her now and again. Send him along one Sunday.'

'But that's what I mean by awkward. If I sent him and he thought we'd been talking, he'd be against it from the start.'

'Then it'll have to be fixed to look like an accident. Maybe it'd be best if I sent her. I know—when we part, you give me fourpence; then I can tell her you gave me fourpence too much and send her along with it. Say Sunday three weeks. I was meaning to buy her a bit of Lindsey cloth. That'll give us time to sew on it. I'll try to get blue.'

'That would be best,' Emma agreed. 'Then, if she takes his eye, he'll walk her home and you'll know.'

Curiosity made me ask how far apart their homes were. Nine miles, less if you knew the shortcuts.

It was all very cosy and homely. They had judged supplies to a nicety. As the last goose went onto the makeshift spit. Amy said, 'Well, home tomorrow,' rather as though she was sorry that this year's trip had ended. But one jollification was yet to come. Somewhere along the road that afternoon, they stopped at an inn and bought ale. And that night, before bedding down in a ruined old tithe barn, we all drank freely. We drank toasts, quite as formally as people of the great world did. 'Here's to a good hatching!' 'May the grass grow green and the geese grow fat!' 'May London grow and the prices hold!'

Then, as the ale went in, softer feelings came out.

'May we all be together next year!' 'Here's to our next meeting!' 'Remembering Anne!' I had heard references to her before. She had been the leader, a much older woman but very tough and spry. And rather strange for, if the story was to be believed, as they herded the geese together and were dipping their feet into the tar which would protect their feet for the long journey, Anne had said, 'I shall lead you to London but Emma will lead you back.' And sure enough, when they went to wake her at Epping, she was stone dead. So now they drank to her memory. 'May I last as long; may we all last as long!'

'And die as easily.'

They had accepted me and trusted me. Emma had lent me coined money so that I could buy corn and hay for Brownie; but I was out of this. They would hatch, they would tend, they would herd their geese and, if God spared them, set out next autumn. And perhaps Emma's Robin would have taken a fancy to, and married, Ada's Mary...

There is always a little sadness in the thought of a way of life, not yours, going on and on without you. I had not felt that sadness in leaving Beauclaire because I had never fully shared that life; this life I had shared.

We all grew tipsy. The ale was stronger than wine. I was tipsy. I took the cup, when it came to my turn—having not provided myself with a cup, I shared with whoever was prepared to share with me—and I got to my feet and said—I can hear myself now—'I drink to you all. To Emma and Amy, to Bess and Liz, to Alice and Ethel. May all your eggs hatch and all your plans prosper. May you...' And with that, amidst a great roar of laughter, I fell flat on my face.

In the morning we all had sore heads. That, and the thought of parting, made us quiet. 'I turn off here,' Bess said. And then, one after another, up little lanes and byways, they all went. Emma and I went into Bures alone. And I felt a change in her; from being the leader of a gay, adventurous band, she was a woman going home to a son who was awkward and to about nine months of hard work.

I had already told her that my grandfather would be so grateful to her and her friends, for feeding and escorting me and lending me money, that he would send money at once. Now she said, looking at the sky, 'You should be in Sudbury before night falls... Rest in an inn there and hire a man to take you on to Baildon.' She gave me a shilling. 'Add that to your debt. And God keep you.' A shilling in those days was a large sum of money for a poor woman to lend—on top of a groat already lent. But I took it, saying, 'Emma, you shall not lose by this, I promise you.'

She said, in an offhanded manner, 'I believe you and I can

wait. I always wanted a daughter... Make for Sudbury and don't talk to men with cockleshells in their hats.'

'Never fear,' I said. 'God keep you, Emma.'

Brownie, quite well fed after days of walking pace, not heavily laden, broke into a trot as soon as I was back in the saddle and we were in Sudbury well before dark. Here I was on my home ground and I felt that I had no need to seek an inn. In the little town I asked for the house of William Deacon who had, I knew, had dealings with my grandfather over many years.

Even with him, there was that little moment of suspicion. It was a time of fraud as well as of open violence. I mean that a maid might take a place in a substantial household and one night get up, draw bars and bolts and let in the thieves who would take everything of value. Or a girl might ask for protection and, once inside, do the same thing. So Master Deacon was suspicious of me—a girl he had never seen, extremely dirty and untidy, riding up and claiming to be Martin Reed's granddaughter.

'I'd want proof of that,' he said most sensibly. And I had proof of a kind—if anyone could read. Whether he could or not I did not know. I said, 'Master Deacon, can you read?'

He said, 'No. I never had need. But my boy can and he is here from the monks' school at Baildon, to keep Christmas. He can read. I will call him.'

He was a small boy, but sharp. I offered him Walter's deed of gift to me... and he read it, word by word... I hated showing it but it was the only thing in the world to show that I was who I claimed to be. Master Deacon said, 'That will do, Thomas,' to his son. And to me he said, 'This is a most sad thing. I felt for him, good, honest man, with his son dead and his grandson run wild. I heard the news with sorrow.'

Then I was taken in and there was hot water and soap and towels, a brush and a comb for my hair, a supper which, now that everything seemed over, I was too tired to enjoy and then sleep on the goose-feather bed, the goose-feather pillow between the linen sheets. I slept as the dead sleep.

81

CHAPTER IX

I shall do well now, thank you,' I said to the man whom Master Deacon had told to ride with me to Baildon, and he was only too glad to turn around and go. The Twelve Days of Christmas were running out and this day was ending early, with a lowering sky that threatened snow.

'If you are sure, Mistress,' the man said.

'I am sure,' I said. 'Good-bye.'

On the wide open space outside the great gate of the Abbey he turned and rode away leaving me, safe in my own home town, to make my way the small distance through the ruined old South Gate to the place called the Old Vine where my grandfather had rooted himself and stayed, built his house and his business, married his second wife, seen his son born, seen him die, had cherished his grandchildren, sent one away to be taught manners and watched the other one take off to be what he felt he was born to be. I now began to think seriously about how I would be received.

Leaving Beauclaire in such misery of spirit, meeting with my misadventure and then travelling in such jolly company, I had pushed the thought to the back of my mind. Now on this, the very last stage of my journey, I knew only one thing for certain—nothing would make me go back to Beauclaire. Grandfather, I hoped, would side with me when I had told him everything; Mother would probably think I ought to return and finish out my time but this time I would utterly refuse—not shouting and crying, as I had done before, but in a way that would show her that I had nothing left to learn.

At the Old Vine, nothing was stirring which did not surprise me, for the Twelve Days were not yet up and apart from

82

absolutely necessary jobs, like feeding animals, no work was done. I stabled Brownie myself and filled his manger to make up for the lean days. Then I went into the house by the kitchen door.

There I did expect to find some activity. Old Nancy had been my grandfather's most devoted servant since those faraway days when he was a poor man, just beginning his business. And she cared nothing about holidays; the young could go merrymaking, she said, but she stayed on the job.

There was no one in the kitchen; the fire was out, everything was filthy and cluttered. Old Nancy was an extremely clean and tidy woman and my mother was fastidious to a degree. Neither of them would have allowed dishes and cups to stand around unwashed. I began to sense something was very wrong.

I went through to the little room where my grandfather spent most of his time among samples of wool and cloth and bundles of tally sticks which served him in place of written records. The door was closed but as I neared it, I could hear a tapping sound and my grandfather's voice calling, 'Girl! Girl!' I opened the door and went in.

He sat in his chair with his feet on a stool, a blanket over his legs and a shawl around his shoulders. The fire here was almost dead.

I said, 'Grandfather, it's me. It's Maude. I've come home.'

He looked at me disbelievingly, screwing up his eyes and peering.

'Maude?'

'Yes,' I said, and went over and kissed him. He did not smell right. Ordinarily he smelled of wool and of the out-of-doors; now there was something sourish about him. He hugged me and I hugged him; he had grown thinner.

'Are you ill?' I asked, standing back to look at him.

'No, no, child. Well enough. My bad leg failed me and I had a fall and hurt my hip. It will mend. So you came? I wronged the fellow.'

'What fellow?'

'The one who came to teach Walter. When Walter left... I told

83

him to sit down and write to you, bidding you home. And then again, when I took this tumble... But I could never be sure.'

I thought — so they did send for me! That made things much easier for me, seeming to have come home because I was told to. So I did not say that I had received neither letter. Instead I asked,

'Did my mother agree that I should be called home?'

'Poor woman,' he said, 'and poor Maude. It is a sad house you have come home to. Your mother is not... not herself since Walter went.'

'And old Nancy?'

'Ah, that was grief, too. She died last winter.'

I thought this is no time for more questions; this is a time for mending the fire, lighting candles, getting food. I did ask one question, though. 'Where is my mother?'

'She took to her bed.'

Well, in bed she would be warm at least. I could see to her later.

I fetched wood from the pile in the yard and got a good fire going in the little room. By the light of the leaping flames and the candles I brought, I could see how completely my grandfather had changed and into what utter desolation his room had fallen. Dust lay thick everywhere and on the table set within reach of his hand there was an empty bowl with a spoon in it and a cup and a jug, also empty.

I asked, 'Have you eaten today. Grandfather?'

'Oh yes. Not well, but enough.' Something of liveliness, new to me and surprising, for he had never been a lively man, brightened his eyes. 'Lame as I am,' he said, 'I hobble on these two brooms...' I saw them, then, leaning against his chair, 'to the necessary house... and that takes me through the kitchen. So in addition to what I am given, I have what I take. The carrying is the difficulty.' I could see that.

'I will look in upon my mother,' I said, 'and then I will make supper for us all.'

He said, stretching his hands toward the fire, 'Maude, do not be alarmed. With women, when the heart breaks, all goes. They are made that way. Men have other things to think of; they can turn to business. I did.'

I thought—and so did I, woman though I be. Melusine's death, and all to do with it, broke my heart but I turned to the business of getting home, of stealing out of Beauclaire, to the journey, to getting Brownie back. I saw that I had been singularly fortunate. Mother, I thought as I climbed the stairs, had centred her life on Walter and when he left had nothing with which to mend her broken heart.

Her bedroom had always been for me a place of mystery and of an enchantment to which I would not admit. It had always smelled so sweet and there was the table, near the window, full of things no child must touch. Even now I approached that room with care, tapping on the door as I had been taught. No voice bade me enter but I lifted the latch and walked in.

The short winter day had now come to its close and this room was even colder and darker than the one below stairs where my grandfather sat. There was the bed, piled with blankets.

'Mother,' I said. 'It is Maude. I have come home.'

The hump on the bed did not stir. I thought she was asleep and stole away.

Whoever now had charge of the kitchen at Old Vine, though slovenly, had not neglected to provide food. In the larder there was a cold fowl and a cut ham and in the pot on the hook over the dead fire was a stew of hare, onions, and peas which needed only to be reheated.

I threw off my muddied cloak and set to work, slowly and awkwardly at first, for in all my life I had never done kitchen work. I made the fire and while the stew heated I scoured some plates with water and wood ash, as I had seen Nancy do. I cleaned a ladle and some knives and some spoons. Everywhere I looked I saw signs of waste and bad management: bits of bread gone mouldy, milk turned sour, fat that smelled rancid, a pot of something—broth or gruel—so old and rotten that it fermented, hissing and bubbling. It was more than I could deal with at the moment. When the pot was hot I ladled—with the clean ladle—two good portions into two clean platters, set them, with bread and salt, on a serving tray and carried it into my grandfather's room.

He said, 'I am sorry that you should have to wait upon me at the end of such a long journey. But this smells good. And it is the kind of thing I could not help myself to, balanced on two brooms.'

He ate with appetite. So did I. Presently I said,

'Who took Nancy's place in the kitchen?'

'Girls,' he said. 'Sometimes one, sometimes two. They do not stay long; at least not lately. Not since I was laid up. No proper hiring and I doubt about proper treatment. For all he is so clever, he has no skill with people.'

'Who is he. Grandfather?'

'Nicholas Firman, the man I hired to teach Walter. Sometimes I wonder...'

'What?'

'Whether that was wise. And yet, had he not been here, the business would have suffered. Child, there are two faces to everything. I sometimes wonder whether he encouraged Walter to do what he did. And whether... No matter. Maybe I wrong him. He wrote the letter that brought you home to gladden my eyes. I was wrong in thinking that he did not write; I may be wrong in other things.'

'What things?'

'I must not trouble you, Maude. Once I am over this I shall get things into order again. You must not worry. You arrived at a bad time and you must rest.'

'I shall, presently. How do you manage the stairs?'

'I cannot. I sleep here.'

'In a chair! Why was a bed not brought down?'

'It was tried. It stuck at the turn of the stairs and could come no farther.'

'A new bed could have been brought in.'

'That would have been to make a great fuss about nothing. And tongues wagging everywhere—poor man, he is abed in a downstairs room. I did not wish that. I am mending, somewhat slowly, but mending. I wait for the better weather.'

I pretended—being skilled now in pretence—to change the subject. 'Is Jack Plant still in the yard?' I knew the answer. Jack Plant would never have allowed my grandfather to be so neglected.

'No. That was a blow too. There was some dispute, almost as soon as I was laid up. It was natural enough, I suppose. Jack had always been my right-hand man and perhaps he thought he should have taken the reins. But he was a horseman, not a sheepman. They had some stupid little quarrel about the pack ponies' fodder and Jack flung off.'

'A pity,' I said, and changed the subject again. 'When you fell, did you have the doctor to see you?'

'Yes. And much good he was! Talked to me as though I were a baby. He told Master Firman what we both knew—that I was old and must rest and be patient. And he left some soothing drops to dull the pain. But I have seen what they can do!'

'In what way?'

'Well,' he said, and hesitated. 'Now that you are home, Maude, you must know. Your mother's trouble started that way. You see, Walter's going shocked her. It did not shock me—he had spoken of it often enough, and I knew that sooner or later... When he went she was like a madwoman. The doctor came and gave her soothing drops and now, poor soul, she cannot live without them. Them and wine. She is in a very poor state. You will see a sad change...'

'This man who came to teach Walter, is he a sheepman?'

'Yes. Luckily. Born to the trade but a younger son, so sent to school. His father wanted to make a priest of him. And that was not to his liking, so he came to teach Walter and taught him well, in everything but good sense. Then, when Walter left, he stayed on... And since my fall... well, where should I have been without him?'

'Where is he now?'

'Making merry with some friends. Out Nettleton way, I believe.'

'Leaving you alone like this?'

'It seldom happens quite like this. One must make allowance

for the season. I am sorry that you had such a poor welcome.
For that we must make up when I am about again.'

With that he pushed the rug from his knees and reached for
the brooms. It was painful to watch him heaving himself up but
when I offered help he said, 'No. Short of a giant to pick me up
bodily, help hurts more than it helps. I manage.'

'You should have a stool in here.'

'And who would empty it? Girls will cook, after a fashion,
because they like to eat. Nothing else gets done.'

I thought—something will be done now! As soon as he had
dragged himself away, I ran upstairs. Outside his bedchamber
I stopped; his bed, not slept in for weeks, would need airing
before it was fit to use. But Master Firman presumably had slept
in his bed last night, so I took his good goose-feather mattress
and, partly by pushing, partly by pulling, got it downstairs and
spread on the hearth in my grandfather's little room. Pillow and
blankets I took too.

He was so pleased and touched when he saw it that I was
angry that no one had thought to provide a bit of comfort for
an ailing old man.

I said, 'Why did you not order this to be done?'

'My dear, unless you are able to see that an order is obeyed,
to give it is worse than useless. It merely makes for ill feeling.'

He sat first in the chair, then lower on the stool and then, very
gently, eased himself onto the bed. 'I am more comfortable
already,' he said. And of course, for a man with one lame leg
and an injured hip to sit cramped, day and night, was the very
worst thing. Anybody who could allow it was either hard-
hearted or wicked or both.

In my own, much longer unused and unaired bed I dared not
sleep. So I took the rug that had lain on my grandfathers knees
and, wrapped in it, slept on the floor which was no harder than
the ground I had slept on with the goose-women. But I slept
less well. Too much was going on in my mind.

I thought about the letters. One sent when Walter left and
the old man wanted me, his remaining grandchild, home. One
sent in October, after his fall, when he wanted someone of his

own family, sensible and active, about him. I had had no letter.
I very much doubted whether either had been sent.

Why?

Because Master Firman had not wanted me home.

I thought how strange it was that from Beauclaire I had
always looked back upon the Old Vine as such a well-ordered,
comfortable place and how, in my deep misery over Melusine's
death, I had looked upon it as a place of refuge and had made
my way toward it, not quite sure of my welcome but sure that it
would be as I had left it. And what had I found?

Finally, exhausted, I drifted toward sleep and remembered
something as one does between sleep and waking. It was a bit
of nonsense from those childish games. Henry Rancon was
saying gruffly, 'Sir Reed, the enemy must be outwitted.'

CHAPTER X

Falling asleep so late, I overslept in the morning. I dreamed toward the end of my sleep that the goose-women had stolen out of the chalk pit and left me alone. So I woke in a panic and there I was in my own bedroom, in my own home.

When I left for Beauclaire, among the things my mother thought necessary was an ivory comb, so the old bone one still lay on the shelf. I used it hastily and then ran down. My grandfather was still asleep. I closed the door softly and equally softly opened the door to the kitchen which was almost opposite. I was thus able to look upon my enemy before he looked upon me.

He and the girl sat at a roughly cleared space on the big table, eating bread and ham and drinking ale. They were talking and laughing together. I was surprised to see that he was so young. I had imagined Walter's tutor as middle-aged at least. From what I could see of him sideways he was handsome, too, with shiny black hair dressed in the fashionable style, ear length and the ends turned under, a good straight nose and a rounded chin. He was well clad, in a dark-mulberry-coloured tunic and hose. Of the girl I could see little, since she sat on his far side.

He said—and his voice was pleasant, 'You cut it for me; it tastes sweeter that way.' She said, 'So now I must feed you as though you were a tame rabbit. My little bunny; my funny little bunny honey.'

I said, in my best Dame Margery voice, 'Good morning!' If a ball from that new weapon, the cannon, had fallen on the table before them, it could not have startled them more. They both sprang to their feet and turned to face me, oversetting the bench on which they had been seated.

Somebody once told me that the person—man or woman—who goes red in the face when angered or embarrassed is harmless. The one to beware of is the one who whitens. The girl—not that she mattered much—went fiery red; he turned the colour of badly bleached linen. But he recovered from his surprise quickly and said, 'Mistress Maude.' And bowed. 'You have just arrived?'

'No. I arrived yesterday, just before sundown.' He then said something that told me with what a slippery customer I had to deal.

'So the letter I wrote reached you.'

A year and a half ago I should have raged at him, telling him bluntly that he had written no letter; but I had learned. In games of skill, a good card should not be thrown down too soon. So I simply said, 'I am here. For my grandfather my arrival was timely. Except for my mother, he was alone in the house and his fire was almost dead.'

'Oh,' he said, 'surely not... Polly, you naughty girl. Did you steal out and leave Master Reed untended? Of late,' he said, turning back to me, 'we have taken care not to be both absent at the same time.'

The girl said, 'I did ask. Master Firman, when you left for Nettleton I could not know, could I, that my sister had two fowls in the spit and a cask broached. Her little boy came along to invite me and I left Master Reed with a good fire and food to his hand and asked permission to go.'

The man said, 'I am sorry indeed that your welcome home was so poor. Mistress.'

Those childhood games, silly as they may have seemed, again served me. 'Attack at the weakest point.' 'Gain an ally if you can.'

The girl was the weak point here. She was pretty in the way that all girls of her age, not cursed with a harelip or badly pocked, are pretty—a lot of brown hair, bright eyes; inside the bodice, not properly laced, a full white bosom. To her I said,

'Things are in a bit of mess here.' The words were mild but the glance I cast over the mess was strict. 'Is it that you are

91

unable to deal with it? Because if so, I must at once begin to look for someone older and with more experience.'

'Oh no,' she said. 'No, Mistress. I can manage, I swear. It was just the season. All will be sweet and clean by midday.'

Master Firman said, 'I always said you were a sloven, Polly.'

I should have thought it impossible for her to turn even redder but she did and she threw him a dirty look. I noted it with pleasure.

'I also have work to do,' he said and slipped away. I wondered what sort of mess I should find in the yard and weaving sheds; but I need not have worried. A man tends to look after what is his own and with Walter lost, me at Beauclaire, my grandfather housebound and my mother taking no interest, Nicholas Firman looked upon the Old Vine as his own already.

I went again to my mother's room and this time found her awake, out of bed, clad in a loose robe of wool and a pair of slippers. She had been such a pretty woman and now there was no trace of beauty left. Her eyes and cheeks were sunken and her expression set in lines of hopeless misery. Had I met her in the street I should not have recognised her. She stared at me with a vague, dull look.

'It's Maude, Mother. I've come home."

'So I see,' she said after a pause, as though her mind needed time to take in even such a simple piece of information and find words to reply to it.

'I am sorry that you have been ill,' I said, thinking it best not to mention Walter yet. 'But I'm here to look after you now. I am going to make bread and milk for grandfather's breakfast. Would you like some?'

After another pause she said, 'No.'

'You would feel better...'

To that she made no answer and, since I had so little time to waste just then, I left her.

Downstairs again. My grandfather awake.

'The best night I've had since it happened,' he said. 'But how, from this position, do I get upon my brooms?'

'With help,' I said. I called Polly and between us we heaved him up, from bed to stool, from stool to chair, from chair to crutches.

While he was gone I made his bread and milk, remembering that he did not like it sweetened with honey but salted and lightly peppered.

'This is good,' he said, 'this is very good.' When he said that, Polly was kneeling on the hearth, getting his fire going. She turned her head and said, half-sulkily, half-apologetically,

'I'd have made it for you. Master Reed, if I'd been told.'

'Yes,' he said, 'I've no doubt you're a biddable girl.'

He had never, as I remembered, been a man to say much but every now and then he could say, in few words, something that would have taken another man a hundred. That simple sentence contained much meaning.

When the fire was going brightly, Polly went back to the cleaning of the kitchen and my grandfather said,

'He is so ready of tongue. He told her, I have no doubt, as he told me, that for me to eat little in my state was a good thing. Less weight to heave about.'*

'And less spirit,' I said, thinking how Brownie and I were both flagging when we fell in with the goose-women.

'True. With a good supper and a good breakfast and a sound night's sleep, I am twice the man I was yesterday at this time.'

'And tomorrow,' I said, 'you will feel twice the man you are today. Later on, when I have seen to the airing, you shall have a change of clothing. And tonight you shall sleep between sheets.'

'It is a heavy burden for such young shoulders,' he said. 'But, Maude, there are still good people to be hired. With every step so painful, I could not go and hunt.'

'I will, presently.'

He spooned up the last of the milk. Then he said,

'Have you seen your mother?'

'Yes. I offered her breakfast. She refused it. I shall try again at dinnertime.'

'It may not work. You must not mind failure there. Poor Anne, she is punishing herself.'

93

'For spoiling Walter?'

'No. For something farther back. I never knew but I think she blames herself for your father's death, for the cold that started his cough. She took Walter's going as a punishment.'

'I have seen Walter, you know. He was very well and very happy—having got his own way. Shall I tell her that? At the proper moment?'

'It might cheer her,' he said. 'It will not make up for the loss.' He sounded as hopeless as Mother looked.

'You miss him, too?'

'As company, yes, now and again. But I knew he would go in the end. I knew from the moment he first took that lute in hand. I'd been through that hoop before.' With my grandmother, I supposed, the gypsy woman who could not stay at home.

I said, 'Well, here I am and I shall never leave you.'

'Never,' he said, 'is a long time, my dear. In four or five years you will be married.'

At Beauclaire I had learned to keep my thoughts to myself, so I made no answer to that.

All that day I worked like a fury and, to give her due, so did Polly. The neglect of cleanliness could be cured, though not all in one day. Much more serious was the neglect to provide for the winter. This year no hams had been cured, no beef or pork meat put away in barrels of brine, no pears or apples sliced and strung on strings to dry, no butter salted down. The ham which was now being eaten was one left over from the previous year and when that was gone we should have no meat of our own. The Old Vine had always been such a well-stocked, well-provided-for place, it seemed shocking that we should be reduced to buying, in midwinter, when prices were at their highest. It was impossible for me not to think that my mother would have done better to have busied herself in her sorrow than gone to bed with soothing drops and wine. Curiously enough, of that there was no lack. In the otherwise empty larder there were several little casks of it.

I did have one stroke of luck that day.

I'd cast my mind back to how old Nancy would have dealt

with the rather dried out remains of roast chicken and, again slow and awkward, had done the best I could from memory. The result, not up to hers but not bad for a beginner, I carried first to my grandfather. 'Chicken and herb dumplings, in case you should not recognise them," I said, and he smiled.

'I didn't know that girl had it in her,' he said.

'I don't know whether she has or not. I made them.'

I then carried the same dish, in a smaller amount, to my mother. As I was preparing that tray, Polly said, 'Shall I carry the jug?'

'What jug?'

'About this time I take a jug of wine. Every day.'

'Thank you for reminding me.' I chose a very small jug and even that I did not fill.

Mother, dressed as she had been earlier and with her hair still uncombed, sat staring out of the window.

I said, 'I have brought you some dinner.' She looked at the food dully and said,

'I only eat when I must. And nothing tasty.'

I tried the cheerful approach to her, too. I said,

'Then try this. My first attempt at dumpling, warranted not to be tasty.'

It did not work. She said,

'Leave the jug.' She looked at it, again with that look, and she sounded as though between her mind and her eyes and her tongue there were a gap. 'Is the other broken?'

In a way it was like the old days, before I went to Beauclaire, when everything I did was wrong and for everything that went wrong I was immediately blamed. I left her with the little jug and carried the dinner down and gave it to Polly.

While she was eating it, somebody tapped on the kitchen door and when I opened it there stood a short, sturdy woman, built like a pony—that was my first thought.

She said, 'It's true then. Thanks be to God!'

That took me aback a bit, and I blurted out, 'Who are you?'

'Jack Plant's mother,' she said; and that surprised me. Jack Plant—to me always a grown man and his mother looking so

95

much younger than mine! 'You don't know me, Mistress, but maybe you remember Jack.'

'Indeed I do. He taught me to ride. He went with me to Horsham. Outside my family, he was my favourite person for years and years.' I opened the door wider. 'Come in.' She did so and looked at Polly eating dumplings at the table.

'Could I have a word in your ear, alone?'

'Of course,' I said and led her into the parlour where there had not been a fire for months. The chill struck and I shivered as I said, 'What is it that you have to say?'

'It is about Jack. Tom Fletcher, he sees to the horses now, he came in last night and said there was a brown pony with pale mane and tail in the stable and Jack said it'd be yours. So I took the chance to come and try to make things right. It was such a worry to me. Jack never did anything wrong.'

'I believe that.'

'Then will you tell Master Reed? It looked so bad. Jack working here all those years and trusted. Then once the poor old man was abed being sent off like that. I wanted Master Reed to know. But nobody could get in. I sent Jack, the very day he came back and told me. I said, 'You go and have a word with the master.' So he tried and was turned away. So then I thought I'd try myself but they said he was too sick. On his deathbed, they said, and not to be bothered. I didn't want to bother the poor man. I don't want to bother you. But I did want Master Reed to know. Jack never did anything wrong. In fact he was holding to what he'd been told.'

'What about?'

'Feeding the pack ponies properly,' she said. 'There wasn't a better-looking string of ponies anywhere till this man took over and started cutting down on their fodder. Jack didn't like that, so he spoke up and got the sack. I just wanted Master Reed to know and I thought to myself they couldn't keep you out and you could tell him.'

'I will,' I promised. 'Tell Jack from me not to worry. My grandfather is not going to die. God willing, we'll see him about again and things as they were...' Saying that made me measure up the load I had shouldered and I said, 'I wonder if you could help me. I need a really reliable, active woman to help in the house. Do you know of one?'

She said, rather shyly, 'Would I do? I can cook and I know the house. I worked here when I was a youngster.'

'There's nobody I should like better. Are you free to come?'

'Not today. Tomorrow. I've got a job for this afternoon. Jack and me have been taking any odd job since he lost his proper one and they're not so easy to come by in winter. A good steady job would be a godsend to me.'

'And if you came here who would look after Jack?'

'Why, his wife. You see, that was the hard part. He'd just married, the end of September, and then this had to go and happen.'

We arranged that she should move in first thing next morning.

She had said that she could cook. But what? What remained of the hare in the pot and what remained of the ham was already cooked. It sounded unbelievable but this steady, substantial household was about two meals away from hunger. At least, I corrected myself, not hunger, for we still had flour and we had dried peas. The peas had ripened and been podded and dried before Walter left and my mother lost interest in such things.

Out of curiosity, I said to Polly, 'What would you have looked to eat tomorrow and the next day and the next?'

She said, 'I don't know, Mistress. Why bother? The mistress will not eat; the master must not; me and Nic... Master Firman... lived kind of hand to mouth. Something always turned up. Like the hare. Today he's at Horringer and no doubt he'll bring something back. Partridges, maybe, or a pheasant. Worst come to the worst, there's still a few ducks on the pond.'

A few ducks. Eat into that few too thoughtlessly and there would be no ducks on the pond. Hand to mouth. Not our way of living and not, I thought, the way of Jack Plant's mother. Stupid as it might sound, I knew that if she came in tomorrow and found us living in this makeshift way, I should be ashamed.

I said, 'I am going out for a little while,' and went to the stable.

I looked at the packhorses and saw that what Jack Plant's mother—she had given me her name, Ella— what Ella had said was true. The ponies were still far from being the wretched, near-skeleton creatures that one did see about and pitied and turned one's eyes from but they were equally far from being the sleek, plump creatures in which my grandfather had taken such pride.

I bridled and saddled Brownie, very frisky after a full manger in his own stable, and I mounted him, still at that moment uncertain where to ride. There were two places in Baildon where there might be food stocked and stored up and to spare. One was the Abbey and the other was the inn, called The Hawk in Hand.

The inn was larger than one might have expected to find in a town the size of Baildon. This was because Saint Egbert's shrine in our Abbey, though less famous than Walsingham and Canterbury, attracted large numbers of pilgrims. The monks' hostelry could not accommodate them all, nor the host of hangers-on, the jugglers and tumblers, minstrels and beggars who followed the pilgrims from place to place. They went to the inn.

The inn was kept by a couple named Webster and the woman listened to my story of the state of our larder quite sympathetically, saying, 'Oh, fancy!' and 'Dear, dear!' But when I asked if she could sell me a barrel of beef and one of pork and a tub of butter, she looked dubious.

'I always keep good supplies, of course. But in this trade you never know what's going to be needed. Anything I have to spare I like to trade for something else, if you understand me. Not money. There's so little to buy in winter.'

What had I to exchange?

'Sound woollen cloth,' I suggested.

'You can't eat or drink cloth.' The word 'drink' sparked a memory.

'In my almost empty larder there are several casks of wine.'

Her look changed to one of sharp interest.

'What mark?'

'I do not know. I am ignorant of such things.'

'If it was the red wine of Burgundy we could do a swap,' she said. 'There's a shortage of that all around. A whole cargo of it went down in the September gales. And the real proper stuff is never very plentiful.'

'I think my grandfather would have bought the best,' I said.

'Then I'll send John along with the little cart and the stuff. If the wine is right, it's a deal. If not, he'll have to bring the stuff back, you understand. I don't want to look uncharitable but you have to look out for yourself in this world.'

'Let him come in about an hour's time,' I said. 'I have another errand to do before I go home.'

I turned Brownie's head toward the little low house where the doctor lived.

CHAPTER XI

'B ut I knew nothing of this,' the doctor said, blinking at me. 'In, I think… no, I am sure, August, yes, August, I was called to the poor lady, your mother, who was so distraught by grief as to be almost mad. I left, in a flask, six carefully measured doses of what I knew would give her a good night's rest. Six nights sleep, I have found, is a good cure. I said that if needed, I would attend her again. I was not called upon. Not until, let me think, yes, October, and then not to her. To Master Reed.'

'And you have not sent more of the drops. Doctor?'

'If you were older,' he said, 'I should take that question as an insult. A proper physician does not give medicine—especially of that kind—without seeing the patient. It would be a very dangerous thing to do.'

'Then where does she get the stuff?'

'One of these people who call themselves apothecaries. They are bound by no oath, so they can sell even poison with a clear conscience. They serve a useful purpose in supplying what doctors need but they are not content with that. They sell to anybody and that is wrong.'

'Is there one in Baildon?'

'Not yet. Though I expect it every day. There is one in Colchester, from whom I get my supplies.'

'I see,' I said. 'May I now ask you about my grandfather?'

'He ails? Such a hardy man for his age.'

'He is very lame.'

'But my dear young Mistress, he was lame when I came to Baildon, all of twenty, yes, twenty years ago. A man whose broken bone set short is bound to be lame, and worse in winter, when even sound bones creak.'

'I know. It is not that leg. It is his hip on the other side.'

He looked puzzled.

'But that was nothing, a slipped joint. I said at the time, a job for Armstrong the blacksmith. One wrench and the ball would have been back in its socket.'

'I am sorry to ask so many questions. Did you tell my grandfather to send for the smith?'

'Of course not. One never frightens a patient unnecessarily. I told the young man who was there. And I left some drops, a large dose. I told the young man to call the smith and have him ready—to give the patient the dose and wait until he was drowsy and then have the job done. There would be pain, of course, but dulled and soon over and no waiting for it, which is the worst part.' He rubbed his chin. 'If indeed your grandfather is still lame on that side, Armstrong for once did a poor job and should try again. It was so simple I could have done it myself but for my physician's dignity.'

That I understood—doctors dealt with medicine, barbers and smiths with wounds and bones.

His physician's dignity did not prevent him from trying to earn another fee. 'If Armstrong did fail and must try again, I will come along and prescribe more drops.'

'Thank you,' I said. 'If necessary, I will send for you.'

'You are full young to be concerning yourself with such serious matters.' I gave him the answer I had used before,

'I am older than I look.' So I was. It was only sixteen months since I had left home for Beauclaire but, what with one thing and another, I seemed to have aged by sixteen years.

John Webster peered at the marks burned into the wine casks with a red-hot poker and said they were right. Carrying each one as carefully as though it were his firstborn baby, he removed them and then trundled in the meat barrels while Betty, his wife, carried the tub of butter. We were not well stocked but at least we had something and when market day came around I meant to ask around among the country women and hoped to find one who had a side of bacon or some dried fruit to spare. Cheese was easily come by.

101

I looked at the beef barrel and knew that it was extravagant even to think of opening it while there was still some of the hare left in the pot, but I felt that both my grandfather and my mother needed tempting food at this point. So I pried off the lid and took out a piece of silverside. Mistress Webster had done her work well; she had chosen her meat with care and preserved it thoroughly. I washed the joint and set it to simmer over the stove. When it was cooked it cut well, tender and with that rainbow shimmer on each slice which is the mark of real silverside. I filled a platter with delicate slices and carried it to my grandfather. I watched him eat for a moment or two and then asked, as casually as possible, 'Did you ever think of asking the smith to deal with the hip you hurt?'

'Child, if it had been anything Armstrong could deal with, the doctor would surely have said so. You must not fret yourself. With food like this and the bed you have made me, I hope to be active by lambing time.'

I only said, 'I hope so.'

My mother was back in bed and seemed to be asleep. This time I tried to wake her but failed. I set the tray down near the bed, thinking that perhaps she might wake and think the cooling beef just tasty enough and therefore eat it. The jug I had brought up at midday was empty; and I took it away. I also took away the flask which I suspected of containing the pain-killing drops.

Downstairs again, I gave a little knock to the wedge I was trying to drive between Master Firman and Polly.

'Tonight,' I said, 'we will all sup together. Tomorrow, with more help in the house, we can have a fire in the dining room and Master Firman and I will take our meals there.'

He had said that he would not be in for dinner but would be back at suppertime and he now came in, very brisk and amiable.

'Something smells very good,' he said. 'I am hungry. I spent the day at the Horringer sheeprun and shared the shepherd's dinner. Very meagre.'

He settled into his beef—like my grandfather, never questioning where it had come from—and after two mouthfuls said, 'Polly, bring some wine. Red wine goes well with beef. You will take a glass with me. Mistress Maude?'

I said, 'Unfortunately things here have come to such a pass that we cannot have both.' I told him what I had done.

'But the wine was mine! Bought and paid for with my own money!'

I felt very foolish.

'In that case, Master Firman, I must pay you and hope that you can replace your store. We had to have meat and only by barter could I obtain it.'

'To replace my wine may take time and for Mistress Reed wine is a necessity.'

'She would be better off without it and with proper food.'

'Ah,' he said, 'you have not seen her in a melancholy fit.' He said that with grave pity. Then he smiled, teasingly. 'Did you barter away the ale, too?'

'No. I gladly would have but there is no shortage of ale.'

'Then Polly, we will have ale.'

I told him that Polly and I had replaced his mattress and spread fresh sheets on his bed. He said that, finding his bed stripped, he had thought that someone had played a Christmas prank upon him.

'At the time of the accident,' he said, 'we tried to get a bed down but it stuck. I am sorry, very sorry indeed, that the thought of a mattress on the floor did not occur to me. Such thoughts come more easily to women. We have lacked a woman's touch about the place.'

I saw Polly shift on the bench and I saw him wince. I guessed that under cover of the table she had kicked him on the shin.

In a voice as pleasant as his, I said, 'There is a limit to the touch that one woman, or even two, can supply. Tomorrow we shall be three. Jack Plant's mother is coming to join us.'

That arrow went well and truly home. White of face again, he gulped down his beef and his ale and got up.

'I must report how I found things at Horringer,' he said, and went toward my grandfather's room.

'My dear,' my grandfather said, 'you have done so much,

in so short a time, that to say one carping word may seem ungrateful. Bear with me… It was unwise to hire Ella Plant. Jack and Master Firman parted on bad terms and ill feeling remains. To hire her… Do you see what I mean? To be honest, Maude—though perhaps I should not say it—I am not altogether sure of the man, he may have been hasty, but the fact remains that we cannot afford to offend him.'

Not yet, I thought; not until you are back on your feet.

I said, 'I see no reason why Master Firman and Ella should ever come into contact. She offered to come and work here. With two abed and the house in the state it was, I could not refuse… Did he also complain to you about the loss of his wine?'

'He mentioned it. But I made that right. I gave him money. At his age I had no idea of what wine was and I never got around to liking it. But times change.'

Once again I helped him to his bed—this time his own, well aired, well fluffed up.

I was halfway up the stairs on my way to my own bed when I heard a low, miserable sound, not unlike a dog whining. I went toward it, my mother's bedroom.

She was out of bed, just in her night shift, no robe, no slippers, but she had managed to get two candles lighted. She was crying in a particularly heartbroken way. And yet she was, in a fashion, more herself as I remembered her than I had seen her since my return. When I entered, carrying my candle, she said, 'Maude! I should have known!' And she cried harder. It was terrible to see. 'Did you take it? The flask with a stopper? Don't bother to lie to me. Yes, you did. I should have known when you brought me that miserable half measure of wine. You think, you would think, that a plate of beef… Bring me back that flask. You had no right… You never felt guilty! I remember. Even when you were whipped for doing wrong, you thought you were right. I know when I'm wrong. I once did a very wrong thing and I knew it. So I am being punished. And the punishment is more than I can bear without help. Bring me back that flask and a jug of wine. Then I can sleep and forget.'

I said, 'Mother, I have seen Walter. He came to see me. He was very well and very happy. And he played so beautifully. Even at Beauclaire people were astounded and he was sent on his way with warm recommendations. He is doing what he was born to do. It is a mistake to think that his going was a punishment for you.'

'But it was. Or so it seemed... You say he was well?'

'Very well.' I did not mention that he looked thin and seemed hungry.

She said, 'I was wilful and young...' And she looked about the candlelit room as though seeking some excuse for having been wilful and young. 'I thought I had escaped,' she said, 'and then when Walter went... I can't sleep.' She started to cry again.

I said, 'If you would try to eat a little.'

'Not meat. Every day is a fast day with me, now.'

'A little bread, then. We have butter again now. I will fetch some.'

'I shan't eat it. I shall eat nothing until you give back my drops and my wine.'

It seemed heartless, but I thought that perhaps if she were forced to do without them, even for one day, her natural appetite for ordinary things might reawaken. I fetched her butter and spread it on the bread; I fetched sheets and fluffed up her bed, which had not been touched for weeks by the feel of it. She did not speak a word to me while I was doing this and when I said, 'Good night. Mother,' she did not reply.

105

CHAPTER XII

Armstrong the blacksmith said in a shocked voice, 'In October! Then why wasn't I sent for then? The longer a joint's out, the harder it is to get back. How has he been managing?'

'Heaving himself about on two brooms.'

'Oh dear. Worse and worse. Still, I'll come and do what I can. One comfort is I can't make things worse.'

He may have taken comfort in that thought; I could not. Nor could I quite make up my mind whether to tell my grandfather what was about to happen, or so to arrange it that he did not know until he saw the blacksmith in his room. On the one hand, I remembered what the doctor said about the expectation of pain being the worst part; on the other, there was the fact that it was his hip. I could not decide. Then I thought that I would wait and see how the drops affected him. If they made him very drowsy I should be spared having to tell him that the doctor had advised this wrench in October.

It was a fiercely cold morning and that gave me an excuse to offer him a mug of ale, heated by having a red-hot poker held in it and further improved by a pinch of nutmeg. Into it I poured all the drops from the flask I had taken from my mother's bedroom. As he drank it I watched him, like a cat at a mousehole. He drank every drop, enjoying it.

'I haven't had a mug of mulled ale since I don't know when,' he said. 'You are a good girl, Maude, and I'm sorry that I didn't see eye to eye with you over Ella Plant. It was only because…' He paused and I saw in him that separation between mind and tongue that I had seen in my mother. 'Mustn't offend,' he said. He fought against the drowsiness. 'Had a good night,' he said,

106

arguing with himself. 'Feel sleepy, why?' And with that he appeared to go to sleep. I counted a few heartbeats and then went softly out and said to the blacksmith, 'Now.'

But even then it was not simple because Armstrong said my grandfather must be flat, on the floor or on a table. A table was better, he said; and he lifted him onto the table. I stood and sweated, fearing that the movement would wake him and he would open his eyes and ask what Armstrong was doing here. But he did not. Armstrong, lifting him as though he weighed nothing, said, 'Gone to pieces, poor man. Eaten away with pain. Nothing brings a man down more.'

Then I looked away.

I suppose there was a comic side to it. The pain and the jerk of the wrench brought my grandfather out of his drugged slumber. He yelled. Then he struck out, a feeble, old man's blow, but it caught the smith squarely on the nose and he yelled. Holding his sleeve to his nose, which was bleeding freely, he said, 'You're all right now. And damned lucky you are. Master Reed. It slipped in like a foot into a slipper.'

My grandfather said, 'What are you doing here? What am I doing? On a... on a table. What is the matter with everybody? Has the world run mad. Help me up.'

We helped him up and he stood. Lopsided as he always stood when not wearing the thick-soled shoe that made up for the lost inches on his lame leg; but at least he stood with no other support than his hand holding the table's edge.

He said, like a child, 'I can stand.'

I handed the smith a towel. He said, 'When I heard it'd been out since October... Why didn't you send for me then? Hopping about all those weeks and losing flesh.' He mopped at his nose and then nodded. 'Maybe losing flesh did no harm. I could get a good grip on the bones.' His question about the delay had not been answered but he seemed not to notice. He said, 'Horses kick at times, I've known a donkey to bite but I can't remember a human patient ever giving me a bloody nose before.'

'It was accident,' my grandfather said. He let go of his hold on the table and, walking cautiously, only the toes of his short leg touching the ground, he went to the corner where his shoes lay, all muddled as on that October day when they had been taken off. He slipped them on and stood straight.

'A miracle, Master Armstrong. Nothing less than a miracle.'

'It'll ache a bit, till it's settled in, but you mustn't cosset it,' the smith said. 'Keep it on the move, a few steps today, a few more tomorrow, and you'll do.'

A slipped joint, properly handled, could be restored, almost, if not quite, as good as new. A mind gone astray was not so easy to deal with. All that day my mother's moods varied like the wind. She said, in a single breath, that she had not slept one wink and that she had dreamed a horrid dream about Walter. She cried and begged me to bring her wine, to give back her flask. She said that I was that worst of things, an undutiful child. She boxed my ears and said, 'Now will you do what I say? Nobody will do what I say, not even Walter.' And so on and so on.

Ella Plant, helped by Polly, cleaned the parlour and the dining room and made a midday meal of the last of the ham, chopped small and wrapped in pancakes. When I took one to my mother she said, 'I told you I do not eat meat now.' But she looked—I thought—rather hungrily at the tray.

I said, 'Mother, if you really believe that in the past you did wrong and that Walter's going was punishment from God, why do you need to punish yourself?'

'Who said that?'

'You did.'

'You,' she said, 'you always could argue the leg off an iron pot. Give me the tray.'

I did so and she flung it down onto the floor so violently that the platter bounced off, spilling the pancake.

'So much for that!' she said. 'Go away. Leave me to my sorrow.'

I thought—this is more like my mother! Another day, or perhaps two, without that drowsy syrup, without the wine, and she would be back in herself. A sad woman but not a madwoman. I cleared up the mess and went away.

My grandfather said, 'I have walked today's few steps, up

and down in my room; and tomorrow a few steps on the ground floor of my house. I will walk the few steps for the day after tomorrow in my yard.'

'Would it not be better to rest now?' I asked. 'You must not be too venturesome on the first day.'

'My child, had I not been venturesome I should still be driving another man's ponies instead of owning my own and the best-looking teams on any road.'

I thought, 'Wait till you see them!' I had actually lain in wait for Tom Fletcher, who had taken Jack Plant's place, and told him to fill the mangers; but one day of good feeding could not make up for more than two months of short rations.

I said, 'Leave the yard till tomorrow. I can see that to walk still gives you pain.'

'Nothing like the pain that hobbling on the brooms gave me, or learning to walk on a short leg. I am accustomed to pain. I can bear anything better than not being my own man. This is the last day of Christmas; tomorrow everyone will be back at work. I need to look around in quietude.'

'I will come with you if I may, then. If you weaken you can lean on my shoulder.'

So we set off together. In the sheds where the wool was stored and baled—wool from our own sheep and from other sources, regular suppliers—he peered and counted and seemed satisfied. So many bales for the overseas trade, ready to be shipped to Amsterdam; so many for Lavenham, Sudbury, Kersey, Lindsey. All in good order. All in order also in the weaving shed, where the looms had been left, late on Christmas Eve, at least all in order on five of the six. At the sixth loom my grandfather paused and peered. The warp threads—those that ran from the finished cloth, lengthwise—lay there in the greying light of the winter afternoon. The weft thread with the shuttle attached, just as the weaver had laid it down, hung idle. The piece of cloth already woven was rolled up at the back of the loom. Not a fat roll, four or five yards at most.

Very much his own man again, my grandfather said, 'Can you take that piece off?'

109

'I could,' I said. I had watched the process many a time, 'but there would be no selvage; the warp threads would curl and nobody could get this piece going again.'

'I am not sure that I want it going... I have always prided myself... Take it off.'

When I had done so, he measured the cloth already woven, not with a yardstick, but holding it between his nose and his outstretched arm—that was his measure. And having measured it, he put it on the scales and took if off again and looked at it with disgust.

'This is not Baildon cloth,' he said. 'Sooner than sell it as such I would burn it. I make cloth to last a generation, not to riddle peas through!' Still holding the offending cloth in his hands, he went and seated himself on a pile of finished rolls and said, 'Last day of Christmas or not, I want John Bonham, now. This is his loom, or was.'

Twenty or so years earlier, when my grandfather added weaving to his trade, it was difficult to hire good weavers in England; they worked in their own homes, in their own towns and villages and were content as they were. So he brought in men from abroad. The real name of John Bonham was Jean Bonnehomme; Suffolk tongues had changed it. To house these hired men, my grandfather had built a row of dwellings, always called The Row. I knew in which one John Bonham lived and hurried to it. The man was there, making merry on this, the last day of the holiday, but when I told him that my grandfather needed him he looked pleased rather than otherwise and, leaving his own door, turned toward the house. I said,

'Not that way, John. He is in the weaving shed.'

'But last time I inquired about his health,' the man said with an astonished look, 'I was told his days were numbered. And when word got around that you were home, we thought it was so that he could see you before he died.'

'He is nearer dying from rage than from any other cause,' I said.

'And I know why. Yes, I know why.'

But my grandfather did not direct his rage at the hired man.

110

'Since when have you been weaving this rubbish?' he asked.

'Since just after you took to your bed. Master. I was just at the end of my last good piece and when I took it off Master Firman came along and told me to rig the loom to make lightweight stuff. There was a growing demand for it now, he said.'

'And you believed that?'

'Well, I did say that that wouldn't be the real Baildon cloth. And when I saw what was being done with it... I tried to get in, to ask you or tell you, Master, but you were too ill to be bothered.'

'I see. What is being done with it?'

'It is not being sold as lightweight for the cheap market. One roll in every six that has gone out lately under our name has been this. Very deceptive. You can't tell the difference by eye.'

'I did. All right, John. Tomorrow set up your loom to make the right stuff. You can take this and tell your wife to make herself a petticoat.'

'It's good to see you about again, Master.'

'It is good to be about.' He heaved himself onto his feet again. 'Now, Maude, we'll go to the stables.'

'They won't please you, either,' I warned him.

He said, as we made our slow progress, 'I should have listened to my own mind. But when you're old and in pain you're inclined to suspect yourself of being suspicious without good cause. I used to sit there and wonder... about many things; and then wonder was I fair to somebody who seemed to be trying to keep my business together.'

In the stables he asked, 'Who has charge of the ponies now?'

'Tom Fletcher. He's a good boy. Even at this season he has come, night and morning, and when I told him to double the feed he seemed pleased to obey me.'

'I always held that the best rule was to put the whip in the manger. I was proud of my teams. Still, they'll soon recover. It is the injury done to my good name as an honest trader that hurts me most.' He brooded over that. 'I never, so far as I know, sent out a roll of cloth with so much as a flaw in it. Flaws will happen but a flawed length I always sold cheap, and locally, so that I could explain.'

We went back to the house. In the kitchen Polly, still wearing her hood and cloak, had just come with a basket. In it lay what we at Old Vine had always regarded as a great delicacy, those dried and smoked herrings called bloaters. We were just too far inland to have fish fresh from the sea. Very occasionally a load would be hurried up from Bywater, always in high summer when the roads were easiest, but the very weather that made swift travel possible made the fish stink. So when we had fish we ate stockfish, which was mainly salted cod, not very tasty. Bloaters were different, fine-flaked and delicious. They were caught and cured at Lowestoft.

'I hope you wouldn't mind, sir,' Ella Plant said. 'It is Twelfth Night and there didn't seem anything much to make a feast of. And Jack helped in the market just before Christmas and was paid in bloaters, so I sent Polly around.'

'She can now run around again,' my grandfather said, 'and tell Jack I want him back. Tomorrow, if he is free to come. I want everything to be as it was.'

Ella's eyes filled with tears and through them she looked at me with a passionate gratitude that I had done little to deserve. I had not argued or accused or pleaded. I had merely put my grandfather in a position to see for himself. Words can be met by other words; words can go in at one ear and out at the other; words can be disbelieved: but what a man sees for himself... Though I must say that I had expected it to be a week, at least, before my grandfather became so active. It is not only knights who are brave.

'I'll spare my steps,' my grandfather said, 'and go straight to table.' I went with him into the room, yesterday so desolate and dusty, now bright and shining with a good fire on the hearth. I saw him seated in his proper place, the big chair at the head of the table. Then I said, 'I will look in upon my mother and join you in a few minutes.'

When a woman shows interest in clothes—this I have learned—she is not lost to life, to sanity, to ordinary behaviour. And Mother, not yet sufficiently restored to take interest in her own was, on this afternoon, interested in mine.

'You look like a tinker's child,' she said. 'What happened to the clothes you took with you and those I have sent since, for Christmas last year and for your birthday? There was a dress of crimson velvet, if my memory serves.'

'Your memory serves well. It was a beautiful dress and much admired. I thank you for it. But it was not suitable for travel.'

What I wore, good sound Baildon cloth was, I admit, the worse for twelve days' continuous wear, spotted with grease where one of those geese on the tripod had spat at me.

I said, 'Mother, why not make yourself beautiful for both of us? Grandfather is at his place at table and his wish is that all should be as it was. And it is Twelfth Night.'

She said, 'How can I dress up and make merry when Walter may be dead in a ditch?'

'Walter is not dead in a ditch. I'll warrant that he is in some fine place, enchanting everybody with his music and his songs.'

'If I could think that...'

'Walter always knew what he wanted and he always got what he wanted,' I said, 'and it was not death in a ditch—it was the free life on the road and admiration from those who realised how well he played and sang.

She thought that over and then said, rather slowly,

'There is truth in that. So how could he live in Baildon, where men think only of making cloth tough enough to last two generations?'

'How could he? So he left. But he will come back to show us that he was right and we were wrong; that is sure. When he is famous he will come home to show us. And he would wish to find you as you were.'

She thought that over and said, 'That also is true.' She sat for a moment, looking so frail, so aged, and sad that, although there had never been a close link between us, all her affection being centred upon Walter, my heart went out to her.

Then she said, 'There is my new tawny, ready for the cold weather and never worn. The last stitch put in the very day Walter left. A new headdress, too, in what was then the latest fashion, or so I was told. But I must wash first...'

113

Speaking of the new tawny dress, she looked toward the cupboard where her clothes were kept; mentioning the headdress she looked at the chest. Back here at Baildon she had indeed managed somehow to keep up with fashion and the headdress gave me a pang—just like that one I had worn and discarded at the bear-baiting, just like the one in which Madge had stood up to be betrothed, just like the one which Melusine...

But that was all an age away. Another life. Another world.

I helped her, for she was actually in far worse physical shape than my grandfather and less valiant. But she was washed and combed and dressed—the gown, made in summer, now far too large for her—and at her old place at the table when Master Firman came in from whatever errand had kept him away all day. Coming through the door with him was the mouth-watering smell of toasted bloaters.

'Tolly said—' he said, looking at us with eyes that did not believe what they saw. Then he said how wonderful it was to see my grandfather able to walk this far. 'Sir, did I not always say that time and patience would heal?' As for my mother, he kissed her hand and paid her the most fulsome compliments. There is something about pretence if people will fling themselves into it willingly enough. Over that meal we all pretended, eating our toasted bloaters, our bread and our butter. I swear, anybody looking in that window would have said, 'There is a happy little family, not actually making merry on this Twelfth Night but cosy, but comfortable.' Only at the very end, when my grandfather looked at Mother and me and said, 'Leave us. We have things to talk over,' was the first discordant word spoken.

Mother and I left, she leaning on me. As I helped to undress her, she said, 'There are stories about people rising from death. Lazarus, is that the name of one of them? I know how he felt...'

CHAPTER XIII

Later on that evening I went to say good-night to my grandfather who sat in his chair staring at the fire and looking downhearted.

'I realise now that I was hasty, Maude. I dismissed him and he will leave in the morning.'

'What else could you do?'

'Kept him and used him, I suppose. A bent tool is better than none. Yes, I should have kept him. Now that I'm back on my feet he couldn't starve my ponies or send out bad cloth in my name.'

'He did worse things than that—more dangerous things,' I said. I blurted out what the doctor had told me, about himself, about Mother, and I ended, 'You were right about his never writing the letters to bid me come home. I had no such letter. He didn't want me home. He wanted you in that chair and Mother fuddled with wine and soothing syrup. I came home for reasons of my own and that put a spoke in his wheel.'

Poor old man, he sighed and said, 'Yes, yes. I see I did the only thing possible but it leaves us in a muddle, Maude.'

'We'll manage,' I said. 'We'll get out of it.'

'Not so easily. You see, my dear,' he spoke humbly, as though confessing to a fault, 'in the last two months he has done things his way—I don't mean the feeding of the ponies and the rest of it… I mean the tallying. I kept a lot in my head, I had a good memory. I made notches in tally sticks. In the packing shed I made crosses or some such sign with chalk on the wall. There's a man named Deacon, for example, a Sudbury man—his sign is a ring with a spot in it. Stuff that was to go to him was put under his mark; when the order was ready the mark was rubbed out.

115

It worked very well. But he said it was clumsy and slow and started keeping records his way. Words and figures in books. You understand me?'

'Yes. In that he was right. It saves a lot of rubbing down of walls.'

'What you don't understand, dear child, is that now I do not know and can never find out who has, since October, had one lightweight roll to six. I want to call in the poor cloth and replace it with good but I have no record in my head nor on any wall.'

'If it is in a book,' I said, 'I can tell you.'

'You can read, Maude?' he asked in an unbelieving voice.

'Yes. It is one thing of use that I learned at Beauclaire. Did nobody tell you? And if you did not know that I could read, why order a letter calling me home?'

'I thought somebody would read it to you, as that man read to me.'

'I can read and I can write and I know the figures for reckoning, too.'

'Then tomorrow you shall read in his books and tell me the names of those to whom I owe a good roll of cloth.'

So that, really, was how I took my first step toward being a wool merchant—through that little room at Beauclaire where Melusine had taught me and Henry Rancon had pretended, for my sake, to be a pupil, and my uncle with his good looks and smooth tongue had lounged about pretending to be in love with her. Let me not, I would think, reading from the books or writing in them, think too much about that, except to be grateful and to hope that God had been kinder toward her than her fellow-men had been.

My second step toward reaching my ambition came when my grandfather found that mounting and dismounting a horse was now a most painful business. His left leg had no spring in it, his right no flexibility. Sweating and grunting with effort, he would get into the saddle somehow, he was a very determined man; but more and more often he would say, 'You come along, Maude, you can hop down...' I could hop down, count the new lambs, see to their marking, carry messages, relay orders. Presently it was understood that where he went, I went. I was no longer needed in the house; my mother was back in control there.

And though the men in charge of our sheepruns and the other people from whom my grandfather bought wool might think it strange at first to see a girl, still fairly young, engaged in such activities, my grandfather was always there, sitting stiffly on his horse, using me as his legs, his eyes, his voice. In the end they became used to me and took it for granted that I knew what I was talking about. Once, when acting as my grandfather's other self, I had gone into a barn to inspect some fleeces that were for sale and I said they were poor and maggoty. The farmer came out to argue the point with my grandfather, waiting outside on his steady old horse. My grandfather gave him a simple answer which pleased me immensely. 'If Maude says so, it is so,' he said.

Nobody could pretend that it was an easy life. It meant getting up early in the morning and riding out, whatever the weather, when most females were in by the fire; but I was hardy and grew hardier. And I had not done when I had reached home and eaten my supper for, once having started the 'book work,' as he called it, my grandfather made no attempt to go back to old ways of relying on his memory and making notches in sticks and marks on walls as a way of reckoning things. But this was my way of life, the one I had chosen, and when one is doing what one wants, hardships and efforts go unnoticed.

My mother thoroughly disapproved of it all. She was still melancholy and resentful of the fact that it was her unfavourite child whom she saw every day. She soon forgot that I had, in a way, come to her rescue and was always ready, as in the old days, to find fault. She was particularly shocked when, after some unhappy experiences, I designed for myself some clothes suitable to the job.

Sheep do not do well on damp ground but after heavy rain or snow even the highest and driest sheeprun becomes muddy. Farmyards themselves are in winter complete seas of mud, so I shortened my skirts—at least I had two short ones made—and I ordered from the shoemaker two pairs of stout high boots. 'Anybody,' Mother said, 'would take you for a goose-girl!' She spoke with disgust but the remark did not hurt me. I still remembered the goose-women with affection and gratitude and admiration. My grandfather—to whom I had told the story— had sent money to them and when Christmas came around again he sent a length of good Baildon cloth for each of them.

Being so busy, I found time going fast. The war, so often spoken about, broke out. It did enormous damage to great houses and great families but it affected us very little. It was fought out between the nobles of the land and their own private armies. We ordinary people just went on with our work. Places like Beauclaire might be destroyed; places like the Old Vine stood and prospered.

I spared a thought, now and again, for Henry Rancon and hoped that he was alive and well and going as steadily toward his aim in life as I seemed to be going toward mine. I had his ring, which I always wore, to remind me of him; I wondered if he had forgotten me....

I was fifteen when one morning my grandfather said, 'Maude, take Jack Plant and go alone. I don't feel like going abroad today.' It was a fine June day, too, and not a long ride or a hard errand. Sheep-shearing had begun and there was a clip of wool at Flaxham to be inspected and bargained for.

'Are you feeling ill?

'No.'

'Does your leg, does your hip hurt?'

'No more than usual. But, Maude, I am tired. I am old. I made nothing of birthdays but I kept count in my head. I am eighty-two and that is a great age.'

A great age indeed; sixty was reckoned old. For the first time it went through my silly mind that the day would come when he would not be here. I tried to speak cheerfully. 'You rest in the sun. I'll make the best bargain I can. And there will be strawberries for supper.'

I had outgrown Brownie, who now spent his time between

pasture and stable, and had a tall horse, a silver grey, a very beautiful horse indeed. Riding him was a pleasure; being trusted to do a job on my own was a pleasure. I still liked Jack Plant very much and in the sunshine, with daisies and buttercups everywhere, larks singing high in the blue sky and the cuckoo calling from the trees whose leaves were still freshly green, I should have been happy. But I was not. Alongside me, all that day, rode a horrid thought and a horrid question.

The thought—My grandfather is old and may not have long to live. The question—When I am old, whom shall I have to send on an errand? To whom shall I be able to say, 'You go.'

There was his house which, even after seeing Beauclaire, I thought beautiful. There was his business, built up from nothing, now thriving. There was his name, honoured because he was honest.

All to end with me? With me, bound in due time to grow old and tired and reach the day when all I wanted was to sit in the sun and think about strawberries for supper?

The clip of wool was good and the price asked not bad, considering how prices were rising. I made the bargain and could have gone straight home but I did not wish to.

'We'll go to Minsham, Jack,' I said.

The house there was now tumbling to ruin. My crazy grandfather had died while I was at Beauclaire. I looked at it sadly, thinking once again of how I had imagined Melusine in it. But I put that thought aside and gave my attention to the flock on the sheep-run behind the house. I spotted two sheep in whose hides the shearers had made little cuts, in which flies had laid their eggs and the maggots were hatching. I pointed them out to the shepherd and told him to use his tar brush immediately. Hot tar killed the maggots and at the same time sealed the wound, so that no other fly would be attracted to it. Jack and I helped to catch the sheep and to hold them down while they were tarred. And while I was busy I did not have time to think but on the way home the horrid thought and the horrid question ran alongside me again.

I cannot say whether my gloomy mood had communicated

itself to Jack or not. We had not ridden in silence—in fact, we had talked about our last ride together and he had said, 'I hated handing you over to him, he had a mean, cruel face.' And I had told him how the Astallon man had behaved to me. Then Jack had told me how Nicholas Firman had behaved to him. We had, in fact, made merry over our woes and the defeats of our enemies. But as we turned onto the downhill slope toward Baildon and the Old Vine, Jack said suddenly,

'It's a lot to take on, Mistress. But we'll all stand by you.'

I said, 'Thank you. Jack. I shall count upon you.'

It was oddly like the liege oaths which great nobles swore to the King and knights swore to great nobles, all links in a chain, all saying: You stand by me and I will stand by you.

I was thinking this rather abstract thought when Jack said, just as suddenly as he had made his promise, 'There's a blob of tar on your nose. Butter will take it off. No, don't pull at it, you'll bring the skin away.'

He took the horses and I went into the house. Ella had a leg of lamb on the spit. In June flocks were not only shorn but culled, there being a limit to what any sheeprun could support, so fresh mutton was plentiful in summer. The roasting mutton smelled good and so did the mint which she was chopping small on a board, to put in vinegar and make mint sauce. But the most powerful scent in the kitchen was that of the fresh-gathered strawberries in a wide basket, so that no berry pressed upon another, still all warm from the sun.

I said, 'Ella, is there butter handy?' It was. I took a little piece and rubbed it into the tar spot on my nose. Then I went through into the passage and my grandfather's door was open, so I stayed there, still rubbing my nose, and told him about the Flaxham fleece and the price I had offered, the bargaining, the settlement and then how I had gone on to look over our own sheep at Minsham.

And he said, 'Good!' and again 'Good!' and 'I knew I could rely upon you.'

I went to clean myself before supper. That I was always careful to do. I always changed my clothes, too.

I had reached the top of the stairs when my mother came from the door of her room, looking neat and fresh in a pale silk dress. In a muted light the marks of sadness and discontent and the passing years did not show on her face; she was still pretty as she stood there.

I greeted her and made way for her to pass downstairs, but she said, 'I must talk with you,' and followed me into my room. 'This must stop. I have humoured you both far too long. Look at yourself! Just look at yourself!' She snatched up my little glass and thrust it into my face.

'Mother, I know what I look like. I am just about to wash.' Indeed the hot water stood ready, carried up while I talked to my grandfather.

'You stink,' she said. There was probably truth in that. I had handled fleeces and live sheep, I had trodden on dung and sweated in the heat of the day. I pulled off my boots and began to strip off my outer clothes.

'When I learned that you had gone out alone,' Mother said, 'I was appalled. Had I known, I should never have allowed it. That is the last straw. It must stop! Are you listening to me?'

'Yes, Mother,' I said, and went on washing.

She was in a nagging mood. She mentioned the freckles on my nose, the sunburn on my hands, the way I clumped when I walked in those ridiculous boots, the fact that I had no figure and never would have, bouncing about on horseback all day; I was ruining my eyes, squinting over the bookkeeping; I was growing round-shouldered; I was growing old: fifteen and more and not a suitor in sight. 'And can you wonder? What man would want for himself or for his son, so unwomanly a woman, a cross between a makeshift clerk and a make-believe wool merchant? How can I ever hope to find a husband for you?'

I had had quite a busy day, with my own mind gnawing away at me, and this at the end was too much.

'Let that be the least of your worries,' I said, in the amiable way which I had learned at Beauclaire and which has a sharper edge than a shout. 'I am not makeshift nor make-believe. As a clerk I improve every day; as a wool merchant I intend to improve every day. And when I am ready to be married I shall have a husband—of my own choosing.' I thought, let's have done with this for once and all. I wiped my hand, clean now, and held it out. 'I am plighted,' I said. 'I wear this ring as a token.'

She was dumbfounded for a moment. Then she said sharply, 'Who is he? And how could you plight your troth without consent from me?'

'It was done in the house of your cousin Astallon who, by your own wish, stood in place of parent to me at the time. As to who he is—he is a young man of good family but no fortune. He was page to Lord Astallon until he became an esquire in the household of an even greater lord. We agreed that when he becomes a knight he should come to Baildon.'

Like our games, it was make-believe—neither entirely true nor entirely false. Its effect upon my mother was quite astonishing, as though in one moment of time I had ceased to be an irritating child and become somebody almost her equal.

'You are a sly-boots,' she said. 'All this time and you said nothing.'

'You were ill, my grandfather disabled. There was so much to do.'

'What is his name?'

'Henry Rancon.'

'Oh yes,' she said, nodding her head approvingly. 'I remember his father at Beauclaire. A good knight. No money, of course, but you will have your dowry. Does your grandfather know?'

I saw then what I had let myself in for—more half-truths.

'I would rather he were not bothered with such things, yet. There will be time enough. At the moment he is feeling old and tired. All he needs is to know that his business is in capable hands.'

'Yours?'

'Whose else?'

'I blame him,' she said. 'There are men to be hired. For that

122

matter, I could never understand why he rid himself of Master Firman—such a civil young man, so helpful in every way and knowledgeable of the trade... I am sure that your coming home had something to do with it. Why do you laugh? I am sure your grandfather saw his chance of making you into a poor imitation of himself.'

'A family business is safest in family hands,' I said, lifting down the bowl and preparing to wash my feet.

'Ah,' she said. 'If only Walter had been different...'

Her eyes still filled with tears whenever she spoke Walter's name.

'He is as he is. And I am as I am,' I said, plying the soap vigorously. I then made an appeal to her softer side. 'Of this,' I said, touching the ring again, 'let us say nothing for a while. Let it be a secret between you and me.'

'Very well,' she said, not displeased at the idea of keeping a secret from my grandfather. So then, to please her, I promised to be more careful of my appearance—to put buttermilk night and morning on my freckles, to put elder-flower water on my hands, to wear gloves more often—impossible as it was to test either raw wool or cloth except bare-fingered.

So we left it there. But I carried the thought of Henry down with me to the supper table. Speaking of him had somehow made him seem real to me, suddenly and in a different way. It linked with my morning thoughts and my realisation that I should one day need someone young and active to carry on after me. It linked also with something else, more important now that I stood on the borderline between girlhood and womanhood—his unfailing loyalty to me and the softness of his lips in his hard, rough face.

The fine, warm weather continued but my grandfather stayed at home, sometimes puttering about the yard or garden, most of the time sitting in the sun, half asleep. One afternoon, however, when Jack and I came home, he was waiting for us, looking alert and lively. As soon as I alighted, he said, 'Maude, I have a message for you.'

'Oh yes?' I said, thinking that it was something to do with

business and guessing, from his manner, that it was something that excited him—a new customer, perhaps, or an increased order from an old one.

'The man was mysterious in his manner and anxious to be on his way. He might have told you more but what he told me I have here.' He touched his head. His manner was mysterious, too. He looked left and right and then said, 'It might be as well to go in.' So we went into his little room and I closed the door.

'Now—this was the message as I received it. There is a great lord who was obliged to live in Normandy, his followers with him. He is now going to Hungary to fight against the Turks. One of these same followers wished you to know that he goes, too, because of the opportunity, and will be a knight within a year.' My grandfather reeled this off in the flat voice of a child repeating something from memory and then, in his own voice, said, 'I have missed nothing. The man asked for you by name but he used no other names, except Normandy and Hungary. Can you make head or tail of that?'

'Oh yes, indeed. It is a message from the young man whom I hope to marry. One day,' I said. 'If he lives,' I said.

'We can only hope,' said my grandfather.

I thought—Henry remembers me. I thought about the messenger, mysterious in his manner and anxious to be on his way. I had heard of his kind. A good many great lords had been on the losing side in the war and had fled to the Continent in order to save their heads. But they had lost their lands. A few of them, however, had faithful tenants willing to pay their rents and dues twice over, once to their new master and once to their old. The mysterious man in a hurry would be Lord Bowdegrave's agent, come to collect what he could from the faithful.

I wished I had been home that day. I should have liked to ask how Henry looked, how much he had grown. I should have liked to send him a message, direct from me. I should have liked to send him money, so that when he went against the Turks he went well equipped. But there it was. I had been absent, tending the business, and I had to take comfort in the thought that when he came, if he came, I should have something to offer, a comfortable house, a thriving business...

My grandfather lifted his hand and slapped his head.

'Maude, no doubt about it, I grow old and forgetful. There was more to it—to the message... Read inside the ring."

I had never once taken the ring from my finger since Henry pushed it on. How had he known that? How had he known that there was need to tell me to look?

I now took it off and looked, for the first time, at its inner side. The heavy, base metal had taken the engraving deeply enough to withstand years of wear. Properly tilted to the light, the words were legible— Henry's family motto: 'I keep faith.'